Lock Down Publications and Ca$h
Presents

THESE
VICIOUS STREETS
2
Pressure

By
Gritty and Raw Urban Fiction Writer
Prince A. Tauhid

First Edition 2024

Printed in the United States of America

This is a work of fiction. Names, characters, places, and incidents either are products of the author's imagination or are used fictitiously. Any similarity to actual events or locales or persons, living or dead, is entirely coincidental.

Lock Down Publications
P.O. Box 944
Stockbridge, GA 30281
www.lockdownpublications.com

Like our page on Facebook: Lock Down Publications
www.facebook.com/lockdownpublications.ldp

Stay Connected with Us!

Text **LOCKDOWN** to 22828 to stay up-to-date with new releases, sneak peaks, contests and more…

Like our page on Facebook:
Lock Down Publications

Join Lock Down Publications/The New Era Reading Group

Visit our website:
www.lockdownpublications.com

Follow us on Instagram:
Lock Down Publications

Email Us: We want to hear from you!

Prologue

"Bring your ass here, you little bitch!" the intruder hissed in a menacing tone, as he aggressively grabbed hold of Charlotte's daughter, Ni'Asia.

He put the eight-year-old in a choke hold maneuver and covered her mouth, as he barged into their home.

Charlotte, the girl's mother, was in the back and had the music playing at a higher volume than she normally would. She didn't hear the thud of the gift wrapped ceramic vase hitting the floor. The malicious visitor dropped it when he lunged forward to snatch up the little girl.

With Ni'Asia yoked tightly in the throes of his arms, the intruder speed-walked through the house, in the direction the music came from. The door to the den, where Charlotte sat, was partially open. She bobbed her head to the beat of the track playing.

The intruder stood in the doorway with Ni'Asia in tow and his metal pistol pinned to her head. He then trained the gun on Charlotte.

Finally, she looked up from what she was doing and took notice of all that was happening. Her reaction was a submissive one.

Charlotte's mouth flew open. She erupted in tears, followed by whimpers and sobbing.

"Please. No," she said in a low tone. "I'll give you whatever you want. Just please don't hurt me or my baby. Please, I'm begging you."

Charlotte was so overcome with emotion, her words struggled to make sense. They'd gotten hung up in her throat.

The intruder then roughly shoved the frail little girl from his grip, down to the floor, next to her mother. The move was so forceful that it caused Ni'Asia to break her arm and dislocate her shoulder. She bellowed in pain.

The madman then rushed over to Charlotte and kicked her in the face with the bottom of his boot. He nearly knocked her out. The mother and daughter were hogtied with the laces taken from the sneakers Ni'Asia had on.

Charlotte spit out a thick glob of blood onto the carpet. She was badly disoriented, possibly had a concussion.

"What do you want?" Charlotte managed to get out.

"Bitch, where the fuck you stashing that cash and the work your nigga, Murder, got you holding for him? I know it's in here somewhere," the intruder spat through gritted teeth.

He then grabbed her phone, which was on the floor charging.

"What name is that nigga under in your contacts?!" the intruder demanded to know. He was determined to rob Charlotte of everything he thought the boyfriend had there.

He forced Charlotte to give him the passcode to unlock her phone, as well as the contact name to Murder. He then gave him a call. The two went back and forth in a war of words. The intruder spat the last words, then promptly ended the call.

"Sir, please. Me and my—"

"Shut the fuck up, bitch! I ain't asked you to say shit!" he stated vehemently, cutting her off.

"Sir. Please. I'm pregnant," Charlotte again pleaded for mercy.

"You think I give a motherfuck about you being pregnant, bitch?! Huh?!" He now spat more aggressively than before, truly having no remorse or sympathy, not even for a pregnant female.

5

He leaned over to bark at her again. "You think I give a fuck, bitch?! Do you, really?!"

The intruder was in a race against the clock and had no idea what hid robbery target Murder's next move would be, or whether or not Murder was going to meet the demand he made upon him over the phone.

He stood tall again. Then he turned and ran back to the living room to lock the front door and to be sure no one had shown up at the house unexpectedly. In a matter of seconds, he returned. He then pointed his gun at Charlotte once more. The music continued to play loudly from the speaker of the sound system. Dude cursed at her more. He was now pissed and intent on tearing the home to pieces to locate anything he could of what he came there for. He strongly felt Murder had something there for him to leave with. Then he planned to kill both Charlotte and her daughter, and set the house on fire. His anger raged.

Boom!

A shot was fired. A head wound was the result.

Part One

Chapter 1

Months Earlier . . .

The day for the meeting of the Philadelphia narcotics distribution network of Gustavo Ruiz was upon them. Murder and the others were eager as ever to be in the presence of one another, to run down a line of hardcore questions, and put to bed the blame being put upon every crew but their own. The hitter on the loose caused them to suffer dearly. And now, not everyone would be able to show up, due to many reasons, or maybe just one.

The time was 10:00 A.M., and all that was now necessary, was for the group text to be sent by the top distro, Major, to confirm everything.

Gourdo, the second in command, behind Highway, along the Spanish network, was dressed and ready to make his way to the restaurant destination. He was seated in his favorite recliner and watching a crime drama on Netflix called *Bad Blood*. The home was one of his low key spots, which no one knew of, other than him. The location was in a township just outside Philly, called Chester Brook. The overweight Puerto Rican hustler didn't trust any motherfucker, and had good reasons not to.

Gourdo enjoyed a light breakfast. Actually, to him, a half dozen cupcakes was a bit more on the healthier side than the whole dirty dozen.

While watching the show, he'd dosed off to sleep from the hangover the junk food caused.

Hiss!

The sharp blade of the assassin's knife sang a fine tune along Gourdo's throat line, delicately slicing open the flesh from one ear to the other. He never saw it coming. He never knew who'd gotten to him. The talented female hitter with a vicious knife game was back at it. Gourdo was the next duck in line to get it, and he got it good. The slashing was an inch deep and carved loose everything along its path. Thick, dark red blood gushed forth. Gourdo's eyes instantly peered open. His mouth flew wide. A morbid gag was produced as he grabbed at his throat with both hands, trying to gain control of the profuse bleeding. It was too late. There was nothing he could do. He was left home alone, the same way he'd been caught down bad. And there was no one near to help.

The big fella attempted to stand to his feet. But his nearly four hundred pound frame complicated things. His cell phone was at a ten foot distance in front of him, on the stand, next to the TV. It was needed to call for help.

Gourdo fell forward onto the floor, now bleeding out badly. His life seeped away at a rapid pace. It was over for him. The last thing he was able to take in was how the sneakers looked that the hitter had on. They were a pair of metallic, royal blue, high top Christian Loboutin Red Bottoms. A silver metal tip was on the toe area. Gourdo wouldn't live long enough to make the description known. He was a goner.

Chapter 2

Gustavo Ruiz, the Colombian national, cartel leader, and international drug lord, had a federal mole on payroll, who worked inside the U.S. Attorney's Office in Philadelphia, one of the primary locations he supplied his product. The mole, a male AUSA, maintaining a supervisor position, tipped Ruiz that an arrest warrant was secured for him, and that federal authorities were now on the hunt to track him down. They were determined to bring him to justice.

Prior to the day, a shipping container at the Port of Philadelphia was seized. There were hundreds of kilos of heroin inside, the purest that may have been captured in many years. The drugs were linked to Ruiz. A worker of his was arrested at the port. He flipped and became a government informant, thus compromising the overall operation of Ruiz's enterprise. The feds had the snitch squealing to them on all he knew. They were milking him for all he'd rat about, including the crime of murder.

A body was found at the bottom of the Delaware River. It was weighted and chained down inside a large duffle bag. The guy was obviously murdered on the orders of Ruiz.

The beef between Ruiz's camp and the Italians over control of the ports led to a war. The federal government was contacted by an anonymous source and made aware of a container, possibly possessing illegal contraband. It was believed that the Italians enemy, The Merlino Clan, was behind the leak to the feds, which prompted the raid. The worst was yet to come.

The timing for Felipe Valdez and Major Appleton couldn't have been any worse. With the seizure of supply at the port, Ruiz not sending anymore product any time soon was intended as punishment for them messing things up. The war with the Italians raging, no money coming in, and now Ruiz making them aware that the feds wanted him transformed the entire heroin trade in Philly to a chaotic situation. Not to mention, a devastating drought was caused.

Ruiz issued an option for his three men—Major, C-Ro, and Highway—to have each and every one of their men suit up and the entire network come together to go five alarm blaze on the Merlino posse, because it was the Italians who were behind it all. The little minor shit that the female hitter was doing wasn't even a factor in the greater scheme of things. Ruiz cared about nothing going on at the bottom of the barrel, even though all hell was about to break loose.

Coincidentally, the mole tipped Ruiz about the legal situation looming over him at the same time that the distros were on the verge of meeting. Change of plans, Ruiz now mandated his three top guys to meet with him ASAP, on international grounds, and for them to bring all the money they owed from past times. It was millions.

Everything was called off with the Philly distro network. This was before the group text was to be sent, advising the meeting would no longer happen.

Gourdo was murdered. Now his people were not seeing or hearing from him. They suspected one of the other distro units was guilty of kidnapping and killing him. Also, G-Code was taken out and no one other than the hitter and one other knew who'd whacked him.

For the time being, the whole pony and dog show had been shut down. Completely. There was no supply to feed the streets. The distro network was in total disarray, with some actively seeking out new connects in New York City and elsewhere, and contemplating potentially changing product until there was a change in tide. It was a mess.

The councilman, Major Appleton, had a potential problem brewing on his hands. The associate Murder, was pissed with dude. He demanded an immediate sit-down between the two. The deal between them was already in process on Murder's side of the equation, with one down and one to go.

Murder was told by Major Appleton that the earliest he'd be able to meet and have a discussion would be in the next four days or so, the upcoming Sunday. Murder had no problem with it, so long as a meeting would be had.

* * * *

Four Days Later . . . .
Murder received a text from Major with the location he wanted to meet. It wasn't to be at his home anymore, as Murder was under the impression it would be.

Major: *Barry, change of plans. New location. Meet me at the Olive Garden for a meal. The one in Langhorne Township in Bucks County. It's next to the Acura Dealership. I'll explain when I see you. Be there at 5.*

Murder: *No doubt. I'm there.*

Murder hit the highway alone, like always. He took the back route, up Roosevelt Boulevard. As he passed the now defunct Nabisco factory, a memory was triggered by his sense of smell. It always came to mind each time he laid eyes on the bakery.

Man, those snacks used to smell so good back then, he thought. *I wish I could have some now.* Hunger pangs cause his stomach to rumble. He set in his mind to be sure to make Major pay like no other, once he got to the restaurant. Murder planned to run up a food bill as part of the compensation for his troubles.

He arrived, parked, and sent a quick text to Major to notify him of his presence.

Murder: *I'm here out front.*

Major offered no reply. He simply got up from his seat and proceeded to the front to meet his guest.

"Hey, Barry," Major greeted. "How you been, my brother? Excuse me, ma'am," he turned to have a word with the waitress. "He'll be having a meal with me."

The maître d' was also made aware.

The two gentlemen then made their way to the table Major reserved. It was far to the back. They took a seat then got right into it.

"Yo, Major, what the fuck going on, man?!" Murder hissed.

"Calm down, my young brother. Let's act like two civilized black men here, shall we? Then I'll tell you what the issues are," Major responded. He'd gone into his politician role on Murder. Major was a good actor.

"Man, look, don't be trying to get all educated on me and shit! Just tell me what's up. Any product yet?! Because I ain't been able to make no money. And my crew, haven't been able to eat either. Talk to me, bro."

"Huh," Major exhaled, being reluctant to speak further. "Apparently, something has gone wrong on the high-end, way up the ladder. The big boss had a family emergency, I'm told, and had to go back home."

"Ok. What the fuck that got to do with the product moving?!"

"It has *everything* to do with it. He felt the need to shut everything down. I know you caught the news lately."

"Man, I don't watch no fuckin' news like that," Murder said, cutting him off.

"Come on, Barry. I thought I was teaching you better than what you're showing. Words of advice, if you want to be in this line of business, you've got to know how to play the long game, as well. The political game. You must eat up all information you can from every media outlet," Major stated.

"So what was on the news for me to see anyway?"

Major pointed and waggled his forefinger at him. "You see, that's the reason why you have to stay tuned in. There was a shipping container seized down at the Port of Philadelphia. It was loaded. Everything belonged to the big boss man. He may be in jeopardy."

"I believe I did hear something about that. There were hundreds of units inside, right?" Murder asked.

Major didn't offer a verbal response to the question asked of him. He just nodded his head. He then spoke more.

"And now, he wants me and the other two to take a vacation. To *politik*, if you will," he relayed.

A waiter approached the table to take their order. Both of them were hungry and could use a meal to eat. The appetizer, all you can eat salad and bread sticks, was outstanding, as well.

They got back to the business at hand after placing their order.

"So what? Once I complete the other thing, I won't be able to meet him then?" asked Murder.

"Our agreement is still in place, Barry. Things just won't happen as fast as you'd like. But nonetheless, they will happen. And we shall get back to making progress." Major reverted to his politician role again.

Murder had to smile at the act. He chuckled as well. He was amused at the public character Major took on. It appeared to be so authentic that Murder couldn't tell rather it was real or fake.

"How long you been practicing on that shit there, man?" He referred to the behavior on display.

"Son, I'm a public figure. My character has always been this way. It's who I am."

14

"Yeah-yeah, nigga. Whatever. But anyway. Your dude, initials E.L., it was a home run. He's outta there," Murder declared, referring to him killing the guy, Errol Lawler.

"Again, I watch the news and read papers, son. I'm aware. And that's not to be discussed at no time. What's understood doesn't need to be explained. You understand, son?"

"Yeah. I got you."

The conversation lasted until the main course arrived. Major paid for everything, then got up and left Murder there by himself. He'd gathered all he needed from the mouth of Murder. His cell phone was recording the whole time, the same as it had been when he had Murder to meet him at his home. Major was always careful to not incriminate himself no type of way. The same couldn't be stated of Murder, because he didn't know any better. He was simply a street nigga, and the streets was all he knew.

Major felt the need to safeguard himself in the event things went south with Murder and the bottom fell out. He could easily hand over all he had on Murder to the authorities and not face any blowback. The wiles and ways of a shrewd and seasoned politician are always to be reckoned with. Major proved to be a veteran at the craft.

Chapter 3

One of the iconic brown UPS trucks pulled up to the home of a Shavika Felton. Someone treated her to a gift online. A surprise. She had no knowledge of the fact. It was something special for the unborn baby she carry. It was a box that was so large that, not one, but two workers needed to handle the package.

Well, what might that be? She thought at the sight of the truck in front her house. *A baby crib, perhaps,* she further thought.

The employees withdrew the box from the truck that contained the gift. They then made their way to the front door of the residence. Two females. Shavika stood at the door to await their approach.

"Hello. Miss Shavika Felton?" the fair skinned one of the two asked. She produced a friendly bright smile.

"Ah, yes. That's me. Someone must truly care about me, I see," Shavika responded in a surprised tone.

"Oh absolutely. You're expecting, I see," the parcel courier remarked. "This is a nice baby bed you have here."

"Yes, I'm expecting. And thank you for your compliment regarding the gift."

The second of the two workers, a dark skinned woman, remained eerily quiet for some reason. She uttered not one word.

"Would you like for us to take this inside for you, as well, ma'am? Wouldn't want for you to have complications from heavy lifting."

"That'll be nice of you two," stated Shavika, indicating she was home alone. No other person was heard from or appeared in the house.

The workers then lifted the box, once more, and carried it inside.

Shavika held the door open for them. Then she stepped in behind them to point them in the direction where she'd like them to situate the box. It was somewhat heavy. Shavika had them take it up the stairs to a room. The fair skinned female continued to make small talk the entire time.

Once up the stairs and the gift properly in place, light skin stood and talked more, complimenting for the most part, causing Shavika to smile in the process. Shavika had her back to the door of the room. She never noticed the dark-skinned worker exit, tip toe downstairs, then, return to the doorway of the room.

No one else here, thought dark skin.

Shavika was originally under the impression that dark skin had simply left the two of them there to talk, and returned to the truck.

Suddenly . . .

Wham!

Dark-skin—Quana—waylaid Shavika from behind. The pregnant female was molly-whopped with a wooden mini baseball bat. She fell face first to the carpeted floor.

Wham! Wham-Wham-Wham!

The sibling of Murder, a hitter herself, bludgeoned the helpless mother to be about the head four additional times, for good measure.

Wham!

She'd drawn back with the bat clutched in both hands and came down with greater force on the last blow.

"Bitch!" she spat.

17

Tatiana and Quana then quickly walked down the stairs, lowered their hats down past their eyes to further conceal identity, hopped into the truck, and then nonchalantly rode off with Tati behind the wheel.

An easy $10,000 hit was accomplished, along with 100 E-pills to go along with it. Tati would split the pay off with Quana.

Previously, Tatiana reconnected with a guy she used to have a sexual relationship with. He'd been also used like hell for money and transportation. Simply put, dude was a lame, a complete square-ass nigga, who knew nothing about the street and had no ability to recognize game when encountered with it, no matter how hard he tried.

Tati gave him a good dick suck the day of the hit. She made up a lie to perpetrate to him. She claimed she needed to borrow his work truck because her aunt wanted to surprise her soon to be husband with a large gift. The present was supposed to have been a large makeshift cake, which a stripper was to pop out from at the bachelor party. She needed his work vehicle to pull off the extraordinary feature.

He couldn't make himself say no to that. Not behind the mind-blowing head job Tati put on him.

She had it all worked out. And now, the work was put in for Murder, clearing the way for him in other areas. But how did Quana get involved? And why would Tatiana mention anything to her if Murder had not, specifically telling her not to mention anything to anyone, not even family? These became the most important questions to the entire puzzle. The plot thickened.

* * * *

A few weeks had passed since the evening Murder and Jermaine held their conversation over the phone concerning G-Code. Jermaine knew, without a shadow of a doubt, the moment he relayed all he had to Murder about dude, he would become impulsive and spring to action. Jermaine was the one who taught Murder most of the street shit he knew, and they'd done a lot of dirt together, in addition to putting many away. Therefore, Jermaine knew exactly what to say and how to particularly deliver his words to further execute the manipulation he was putting into effect. Murder didn't question anything, nor did he take the time to think twice over Jermaine's words regarding G-Code. He simply swallowed the lies then transformed into his element as a hitter.

* * * *

A special visit request was granted to Jermaine and a particular individual. It was someone he was familiar with. The two served time together there at the same prison facility where Jermaine still remained. The visitor was a feminine homosexual who went by the name "Lucy." A legally recognized transgender now that identified as "she," Lucy was Spanish, Cuban to be exact. Hailing from Miami, Florida, but was residing in Philly when arrested.

Lucy had fake ID credentials to pay Jermaine a visit. During the time the two were locked-up together, they had a crazy type of relationship. And to be clear, no sexual acts of any kind had taken place. Jermaine had too much self-respect as an alpha male/man, and a tremendous level of street credibility, to have gone out bad in that aspect. He was pimping Lucy, and provided protection to her, on the strength of payments made to him by her cocaine kingpin brother down in Miami. Lucy also promised to carry out hits Jermaine wanted done. The visit was a physical update on the progress made by Lucy. They couldn't talk hits and about Murder over the phone.

Lucy was already seated when Jermaine walked into the visitation room. As he prepared to take his seat across from her, they locked eyes and smiled. The snickering began at

19

that point. They'd played a sucker to catch a sucker. The trick knowledge was for real.

"G-Code is dead!" Lucy muttered with a snarl.

"That dumb motherfucka. *Hee Hee Hee!*"

Jermaine couldn't control himself from laughing at what he'd pulled off. Lucy couldn't control herself either.

"Anybody know he done it?" Jermaine asked, referring to Murder.

"Nah. Nobody knows. That's a dumb motherfucka though. Ain't he, Maine?" Lucy replied.

Murder was blatantly lied to. He'd gotten it all wrong about G-Code. Lucy, was the one committing all the hits. And Jermaine, was the mastermind behind it all.

"You are doing a good job, Lulu," Jermaine complimented with a smile. "And the Gourdo hit, that was well done, too."

"Am I?" she responded with a smile of her own. She had a seductive tone to her voice. *I wonder is my work good enough to finally have you one day?* The thought flashed through Lucy's mind.

"Hell yeah, you are. And I'mma be out this motherfucka' soon enough, sooner than you may think. Our business gonna continue, too. A'ight."

"Understood. I know you're a thorough dude, Jermaine. I believe in you. However, you owe me money. A hundred K," Lucy stated.

"And you owe me more bodies, until I tell you to stop. Now, I'mma need for you to lay low. Get outta town. Head back home for a while, and wait for me to hit you up with what our next move is, as well as the names of the toe tags who's lined up to go. We clear on that?" Jermaine demanded compliance. "And more than likely, we may have to hit that nigga Murder next."

"No doubt, Papi. We're clear on that. I understand."

"Good. Now I've got to get on outta here before somebody recognize you and put out ugly lies on me. Then

I'll have to kill, and won't be on my way home, like I am now," Jermaine let out.

He stood to his feet and was about to walk away, back to the dorm unit, until something came to mind.

"Oh yeah, I almost forgot. You gotta get rid of them there sneakers you got on and get some new ones. They now onto them," he said, then exited.

He was referring to those metallic, royal blue high top, Red Bottoms sneakers of hers. The ones with the silver plate over the toe area. Lucy's good luck tokens.

The visit concluded.

At the time when Jermaine first put Lucy on the mission to do those hits, one of the main things he had in mind was to do all in his power to not have that meeting between the heroin distros in the network take place. He wanted to create enough chaos and have them warring against one another so viciously, that he could easily swoop in and offer what he thought would be a good solution to bring the drama to an end. Or he could offer the unique level of protection he could now provide. Jermaine was working his mojo in a major way. Murder had not the slightest idea how badly he was being played.

Chapter 4

Charlotte was off from work this weekend. The B-shift cycle of the medical personnel were scheduled to run the facility. She was a part of the A-shift. Her daughter, Ni'Asia, wanted to stay over at Imani's house with Farrah. The two little girls were like sisters. They loved to spend time together at any opportunity they could.

The day was Friday, in the A.M. Charlotte hadn't long gotten up. Murder was to appear and pick her up that day. The two wanted to spend quality time together the entire weekend, in Philly this time around, not D.C. He'd called to let her know he was halfway down I-95. The time was 9:00 A.M. And there wasn't any need for her to be in a rush to get dressed. The dinner they were invited to wasn't until 7:00 P.M., so she was good to go.

Murder reserved a suite for them at the Residence Inn by Marriott in Center City, Philadelphia. He wanted to ensure her stay with him in his hometown would be as comfortable as could be. She'd began to trust his judgment on a lot of things, and was intent on the both of them opening up to one another.

The mentor, Councilman Major Appleton, insisted Murder, and the lovely female he spoke so fond of, join him and his wife for dinner at their home. The wife would do the cooking. Mrs. Lori Appleton, had progressed through the Philadelphia Institute of Culinary Arts with tremendous success, and wanted to extend the Appleton's hospitality to their new-found friends, Barry and Charlotte.

He—Murder—was a night life and real estate mogul. And she—Charlotte—was a medical professional, who was looking to network, make ties, and gain influence with those in high places.

Murder, arrived at Charlotte's home. He'd taken the trip in his Cadillac Escalade this time, not the Benz. She opened the door to let him in. They'd gone for weeks without seeing one another physically, only by video chat. Charlotte had a love for poetry and catchy poetic phrases. *"Absence makes the heart fonder,"* ranked in the top percentages for her. And the distance between the two, actually worked in her favor, poetically and otherwise, the reason for witness protection.

"Hey, Barry. How are you? I'm happy to see you," Charlotte greeted with a sensuous tone to her voice, as she welcomed him inside.

They hugged tightly and tongue kissed. She'd begun to take a liking to those intimate moments.

If he acts right, I just may give him the pussy this weekend, atop the head, she contemplated.

"Hi, Baby. I'm well. Happy to see you myself," he responded.

Murder was the type of cat who had a soft spot for certain females. Although a street dude and a die-hard killer, he was a tender dick, no doubt, for those kind who desired more out of life, as he did. It was the finer things of the upper echelon of society that appealed to him. Ordinary females proved only to be jump-offs in his world, and nothing more.

The two made small talk as she finished gathering everything necessary for the weekend trip. Then they hopped into the luxury SUV and hit the expressway, en route to the City of Brotherly Love.

While riding, the conversation got deep. Charlotte was sure to make mention to him that her girl, Imani, had the hots for one of his homies.

"Somebody asked me to ask you to do them a solid," she let out, attempting to hide her smile, while relaxing in the passenger seat.

"Say *whaaat?!*" Murder responded laughing, already having an idea on who she was referring to.

"Mm-hmm. My girl, Imani. You remember her, right?"

"Of course, I do."

"Well, she's got a crush on your right hand man."

"My right-hand man?" he jokingly played dumb. His smile was maintained. "How y'all know who that is? My right-hand man?"

"We are very observant, Barry, amongst other things. And by the way, what's his name? The guy who had on the Gucci outfit that stood to your right that day, after the football game?" she asked.

"You talking about my homie, Herbert. We call him Herb, for short," he responded.

"So, Herb is his name, huh?"

"Yep. That's my guy."

Charlotte then pulled out her phone and began to text a message to someone. Obviously, she contacted Imani to relay the information on the guy she'd shown an interest in knowing.

"Is Herb your best friend?"

"You can say that. He's my A-one dude and business partner," Murder declared.

"Oh, ok. I'm understanding better now. But I'm curious to know, what exactly do you do? What type of business do you have?" Charlotte asked bluntly.

Murder took a hard glance at her, then put his eyes back on the road. "You want me to give you the full truth about that? Or would you like for me to tease you along the lines of my reality?" he responded.

"Barry, look, ok, here's the thing. You know my name. You know my daughter's name. You know where I live. You know where I work. And you know many other things about me, I'm sure. If we're busy working on being together, we must communicate like that and trust one another. You know some of everything about me, like I've mentioned. However, I only know your name and your age. Now how one sided is that for two people looking to build a solid foundation?" Charlotte put things in a way he'd clearly understand.

"Hmm," he exhaled. "You make a strong point. How could I argue with that?"

"And that's my point exactly. Now, explain to me what the business is you got going, please. You never know. I may be an asset. And we've got three and a half hours to go. That's plenty of time to give it to me raw and uncut. Don't you agree?" She had a convincing way in how she expressed herself, causing Murder to chuckle.

"You're good, Charlotte. And from what I now know, everything to you checks out. I ain't got no choice but to keep shit real with you."

"And likewise, you'll get the same in return, me being real with you," she responded with the same sentiment.

By the time they'd reached Philly, Murder had provided her the business about the business, and left out nothing, except the killings that he'd committed or ordered. He mentioned nothing about his other girlfriend, Brooklyn, either. He felt it wasn't the proper time to reveal that part yet. Locking in good with Charlotte was top priority in the companionship he wanted.

The two went directly to the hotel suite. Charlotte wanted to rest up for a little while. The trip had her somewhat powered down. Murder, needed to make a few errands. He'd gotten phone calls and urgent text messages from Herb that he wasn't too happy about. Unfortunately, someone had broken into one of the storage units they maintained. There was a cache of heroin on reserve, fifteen kilos to be exact. It was all gone. They had an issue on hand to deal with.

* * * *

Four days earlier . . .

Quana and her boyfriend, Heeme, found themselves relaxing and having a much-needed conversation between the two. They'd not long gotten done fucking and were between episodes. Heeme felt he needed more of her time and attention than provided because she seemed to give it more to everybody else, mostly her brother. But he was her man, supposedly.

Heeme also hated the fact that Quana would jump to do any and everything Murder told her to do, a hundred times faster than she would for him. He was the dude who was sexing her many times throughout the week and sharing his life with her, and he didn't really have to. In his mind, something had to be done to fix what he felt was going on in the relationship. To accomplish this, Heeme knew exactly what to do, and her spot, near 8th and Diamond, would be the place to make that happen.

The two were laid back watching a TV series on HBO Max when Heeme called himself letting off the first shot to the play he had in mind.

"Quana, look. We need to talk. It's too much going on between us that I don't feel right about. And I've gotta do something ASAP to put an end to feeling the way I do, even if that mean me letting you go to have the peace of mind I know I deserve," he stated, surely getting her undivided attention now.

Quana sprang up from the bed with the quickness. She sat in an upright position, holding the blanket at waist level. "What the fuck you mean by that, Heeme?!" she countered, sounding as if an episode of anxiety was on the verge of coming on.

"I mean what I said. Something has got to change, because I don't like the way this shit is going!" he responded harshly.

"Why, all of a sudden, now you feel the way you do?"

"Because, Quana, you give your brother way more attention than you do me. And at times, I don't know if he's the one fucking you, or me."

"You better check that shit, Heeme! Like, for real, you better!" she said, now snarling while cutting him off. Her tone was vicious. "Don't get disrespectful nigga!" Quana growled.

"Disrespectful?!" he retorted. "Disrespectful?! You want me to tell you what disrespectful is?"

"Yeah! I'd like to hear your version," she responded.

"Not a problem. Disrespectful is this! How about, the last time you and me was fucking, you get a call from your goddamn brother, that nigga, Murder, and, you stopped right in the middle of what we were doing, jumped up, and then went on to do something he wanted you to do . . . at one thirty in the motherfuckin' morning! That's disrespectful right there, ain't it?! How you think that shit made me feel? Or, do my motherfucking feelings even matter?!" Heeme spat.

"Of course, your feelings matter to me, babe. And the reason that happened the way it did that night, unfortunately, there was something very important he needed me to do," Quana replied, defending herself.

"So, you mean to tell me, it just had to be *you* he could call upon? Nobody else? Not nobody he could've called upon to handle that for him?"

Quana shrugged her shoulders. "Obviously not."

"You see. And you wonder why I feel the way I do? And by you even talking back to me, that shit disrespectful right there!" he blasted on her more.

Quana did manage to pipe down a tab and wasn't so combative.

"So what is it you really wanna do to make this right? How you feel it should be, Heeme? Because your motherfuckin' ass, ain't going nowhere on me, nigga! On God, you ain't! It'll be over my dead body before you do. And I mean that shit," she spat emphatically.

"What I want—"

"Yeah! What do you want?!" She asked, cutting him off.

"Here's what I want. I want, us to keep shit all the way real with one another, Quana. We need to get something going and have some type of business about ourselves together. We ain't got a damn thing established in that area."

"Last I checked, we straight money-wise. Ain't we?"

Quana simply had to rebut most everything he was saying. She couldn't make it her business to shut the hell up for a moment, to allow her dude to properly express how he was feeling and what they could do to fix it. And not only that, she found herself still snarling like an angry female Pitbull. This bitch was a handful.

"Yeah, we are, as two separate people. I got *my* shit. And you got *your* shit. But what we got together? Not *jack* shit. And I got a problem with that, quite frankly, I do" Heeme stated in a way to make her realize his point.

"Huh," Quana exhaled. "Nothing, I guess. We ain't got nothing together."

"And you actually got the nerve, to think I'm the type of nigga who gonna sit around and not have shit going on with any bitch I got in my life? A girl I fuck with? Nah. That ain't gonna happen. Now you got an option. Either we make something happen, like right now this day, or . . . I got two words for you, Quan . . . I'm gone! Now have it your way, sweetheart. What's it gonna be?" he spat, then made a move to get out the bed to get dressed, and potentially leave.

"Oh no the fuck you won't, Heeme!" Quana jumped off the bed and grabbed him tightly by the arm, pulling him to her. "I told you, nigga, you ain't going no motherfuckin' where! The fuck wrong with you?!" she let out. "Stop playing with me, Heeme!" Quana barked. Her face was balled up tightly, eyes squinted, and lips poking out. Shorty was pissed off.

"Well then, what the fuck we gonna do?" Heeme demanded to know.

Quana took a long pause. She finally responded directly to his question. "What you wanna do, Heeme? That's the better question. And you're the man. You tell me what to do."

"You damn right, I'm the man. And that's how the fuck I wanna hear you talk from here on. That way, ain't no misunderstanding about who's in charge of this relationship. Ok?"

"Okay, baby. Now what you got in mind to do?" She was now eager to hear him out.

"I want us to set up shop and start getting money, like your brother doing. I want us to set up the same type of system. Now tell me, how he got things laid out?" Heeme asked. "Because that nigga really got his shit together, baby. And you'll now have two people in your life you highly respect, and who are moving the same way. So if it's anybody who knows how your brother is moving and doing things, it's you, of all people. Dude ain't never got knocked, not to my knowledge. I wanna be the same way," Heeme said, gritting his teeth and mean mugging at the same time for emphasis.

"Heeme, you're gonna have to put in a lot of work to get to my brothers level."

"And what the fuck I got you for again," he retorted sarcastically.

"I'm just saying—"

"What the fuck *are* you saying? Because that's the very last time you gonna put that nigga before me, Quana. Brother or fucking not, I don't give a shit!" he cut her off.

"It ain't even like that," Heeme. It really—"

"What the fuck is it then?! Because I need to know," he let out, then paused for a response. "As a matter of fact, your ass, about to choose sides right now, who your loyalty is to the most. Because I gotta be able to trust you," Heeme laid out an ultimatum.

What was Quana to do? Who would she choose?

Tears welled up in Quana's eyes. Brief pants and sobs followed.

Heeme, maintained his stern look. He was serious as ever. "I don't give a fuck because you call yourself crying. That shit don't mean nothing right now. Murder don't know you like I know you. And I don't think he knows that I put you before anybody or anything. But I bet he won't put you before anybody or everything. Now will he?"

Quana kept quiet and didn't say anything. She simply held her head low and looked down at the floor.

Heeme continued. "I gotta be able to trust you, Quana."

"And you can, Heeme. Don't you?"

"Maaan, fuck no! I don't trust you like that! Your ass gotta earn that shit. The fuck wrong with you?!"

Quana, now truly hurt behind Heeme's words, had tears pouring down her face. The pants and sobbing increased as well. "So what I gotta do to prove I'm loyal to you as my man?" she asked.

"I don't want you to prove you're simply loyal to me. I want you to prove your loyalty to me and *only* me. That means, putting me over any and everybody else," he demanded.

"Will you please just tell me what need to be done?"

"I want you, to tell me everything, Quana. What all is it you do for your brother, specifically? I wanna know how he got his whole shit set up. How he be stashing shit. How he move shit around. Everything. And don't call yourself bullshittin' me either, Quana. I wanna know."

Quana lowered her head as she paused before offering a reply. Reluctantly, she then began to give her boyfriend the rundown of her brother's operation; what part she played; the locations she made pickups of cash; the whole nine yards. Most important of all, Heeme, paid close attention to the details of certain locations Quana put emphasis on. She mentioned *storage units,* where she claimed Murder kept laundry detergent, bleach, and other materials to supply the many laundromats he owned. She mentioned that the storage spots were off limits to everybody, except for the right hand man, Herb. She'd made money pick ups at his place before too

Heeme, knew that Herb was the number two in command of the crew. And since Murder made it to where Herb was the only one who wasn't off limits to those spots, all he had to do was, get Quana to reveal where he lived, follow dude to know the location of the units and the unit numbers, and then, proceed from there with his plot. And more than likely, the first of stops, which Herb makes once he leaves home, was to the spot where he had product stashed, at the storage units, Heeme speculated.

Heeme quickly got busy on the work he now had on hand. The next day after gaining information out of his gullible girlfriend, he set out on the mission, looking to complete the job.

Also, Heeme wanted to know why Murder was taking trips to DC so suddenly? However, Quana made him aware of everything important and all in between, but she never mentioned anything about DC.

As Heeme predicted, Herb left his house and made a stop by a storage unit one day. This was the day prior to Murder and Charlotte being invited to dine with the Councilman, Major Appleton, and his wife, Lori.

Heeme followed. Herb stayed inside the storage shed for twenty minutes maybe, then, came out. He had a mini duffle bag tossed over his shoulder. It appeared heavy. Like it was loaded with something.

"Jackpot. Got your motherfuckin' ass now, nigga!" Heeme said to himself in soliloquy. He looked on at a distance through a pair of binoculars from where he was hiding out.

Heeme left and returned two hours later. He broke into the spot. His immediate thoughts went back to the words Quana mentioned on all Murder kept inside the storage units, at least from what she knew. He kicked over a few items in his search. His instincts went to work to help him properly think. *Where would he stash heroin or coke, if he had the same set-up?*

There were multiple large cardboard barrels inside. Heeme popped off the top of them all to see what they contained. The ones loaded with powered laundry detergent, he pushed over to the floor. He discovered exactly what he'd came for. Kilos of heroin was wrapped tight and situated within the detergent. They were at the bottom of the barrels, fifteen total.

Heeme, made a knapsack from a sheet that was there. He tossed the kilos in it and got the fuck on about his business. There was no one to witness who had weaseled Murder and Herb out of the product that was stolen from them. No one, had paved the way to help Heeme become street rich. He did so himself. It was all made a possibility at the expense of the kingpin brother of his girlfriend. Heeme's come up was becoming from that point.

Chapter 5

Presently . . .

Murder and Herb met up at his apartment where the studio was situated. A decision was needed regarding the heroin that was stolen. What was they going to do about it? And who was it that they think might have stolen their product? Those fifteen kilos were the very last of what they had. Actually, there was eighteen, but Herb took three the same day.

Herb was already there by the time Murder arrived. He had a key himself.

Murder burst through the door demanding to know what happened. "What the fuck happened, Herb?!"

"Bro, I can't even begin to tell you what the fuck happened. Because I don't know. All I do know is that, yesterday, I went to the spot and took out three bricks to supply the trap houses. Then, I went again today, to load up again. The lock was cut. I opened it and noticed all the barrels inside had been pushed over. The work was gone. I can't even begin to tell you who I think probably got us, because I don't know that either," Herb stated.

"Bro, we been keepin' our shit there in that spot for the past year or so now, and ain't never had any problems. Why now? We gotta find out who the fuck got us," Murder stated.

"If I had any idea, I'd be out there right now doing something about it. This shit gonna hurt us in a way," Herb said.

"Fuck! It damn sure is. This is bad timing, Herb. Bad timing," Murder let out. "I had a conversation with the supply man, and he explained to me that the connect got major problems himself. He had to shut shit down. That's why the meeting between the distros didn't happen. Ain't no supply right now. The whole network got issues up and down the chain of command. But, I'm supposed to meet up with the nigga tonight," Murder informed Herb.

"So them fifteen, was the last of it all for the time being, huh?" Herb asked.

"Unless we get lucky in between, and find another connect."

"Shit, nigga! We better get busy trying to locate two motherfuckas then! The motherfucka' who stole our shit! And, the motherfucka who we need to provide us more supply!" Herb stated, revealing exactly what was on his mind.

"My mind definitely set on trying to find out who the fuck stole our shit. But we gotta get on the right track first though."

"That might be a hard thing to do, or, it may not be. We can start by asking the people who work there if they saw anything or anybody suspicious. Better yet, we can ask them to run the cameras back for us," Herb suggested.

"Only to have them make a report to the cops, that our shed got broke into? The one that we keep laundry supplies in, that ain't worth anything too much? The one where we stashed our *heroin* supply? How well you think that shit gonna go over?" Murder gave his perspective.

"Damn. You're right. But look, I'm sure whoever got our shit gonna expose their hand some type of way. More than likely, the nigga gonna turn new money and let it be known. They always do," Herb remarked.

"It's too many niggaz in the city with weight, bro. And, who's to say that the motherfucka who yanked us for our shit, is even from Philly? We don't know where to start or who to blame."

"Murder," Herb spat to get his full attention. "That was fifteen bricks of *Boy* we talking about, bro. Not to mention the drought we now under. I ain't letting that shit go so easily. On my momma, I'm not."

"And I ain't either. But, we gotta be logical too, bro. We've gotta think our way through this one," Murder stated, making it make sense for his partner in business.

"So what are we supposed to do in the meantime, bro?" Herb frankly asked.

"To be honest, we ain't got no choice but to sit tight and wait for the main plug to open things back up again. Or, go out and try to find a new connect. Or, we could consider changing product for the time being." Murder gave a response Herb hadn't anticipated.

I been trying to tell you for the longest, nigga. You selling the wrong product. That China White shit is what we want. The words of his dope head uncle flashed through Murder's mind. Shit! We may need to take a trip up to New York City and try to find a connect to that *China White* shit that my people Dollar Bill spoke to me about, he'd though.

"Switch up the product to what?" Herb pushed back. "Ain't no money like dope money, bro! And this, we know to be true."

"Look bro, we'll get into this at a later time. I gotta go for now. I'll hit you up tomorrow on this. But in the meantime, just continue to be cool. We're gonna get down to the bottom of this in due time. I'm sure we will," Murder said and gave his homie dap. He then left to head back to the hotel suite where Charlotte was, so they could get dressed and meet up with Major and his wife Lori for dinner.

Chapter 6

Murder made a second pit stop by his penthouse before returning to the hotel. He retrieved the gift he had for Charlotte. The plan was to make her feel really special for the days he had her in his company, appreciated as well. In his mind, there was a need to make things solid between them. Material things needed to be added to the equation. These particular gifts he had on hand, should do well.

Now back in her presence, he offered what he had to give.

"Barry, this is so nice of you. I love it," Charlotte expressed with a lot of excitement at the sight of the diamond encrusted, heart shaped, gold locket necklace.

"You like it?" he asked.

"I love it, Barry. God knows I do."

"Come on. Let me put it on for you," he offered.

She put her back to him so he could connect the necklace.

Charlotte hadn't too long gotten out the shower. She only had on her white colored bra and panties set. Upon situating the piece properly, he smacked her on her thick round butt.

Whop!

"That thing know it looks nice to me," he complimented.

She turned back around to face him. They locked eyes in the moment. "Oh, it is," Charlotte returned with a sensuous smile.

"Hell yeah, baby. So nice it makes me wanna put a ring on it," Murder responded, then reached into his pocket to bring something else out.

Murder presented her with a gold five karat diamond ring to match the rope chain. "This for you as well. A promise ring, if I may," he let out, then gently grabbed hold of her hand and began to situate the rock on her finger.

"Oh-my-*effen*-God, Barry. You didn't," she acted, full of excitement now. Her body language and facial expressions were more ecstatic than they'd been in a long time.

Neither Vershon nor any other dude has ever gone to this extent to please me. I'm gonna really give it all I've got with this dude here. He's a keeper, Charlotte had thought.

They tongue kissed intensely. The time of hour came to their minds. The private dinner was in an hour to be exact. They didn't have time for anything else but to get dressed and leave, not even an opportunity to get off a quickie.

Once draped in proper attire, they were out, headed to the home of the councilman and his family.

Murder and Charlotte arrived at the mini mansion of the Appleton family. They exited the Escalade and made their way to the front door. The two held hands. Charlotte had on a stunning, form fitting dress. Black in color. It had an open back to it. She also had on a pair of Christian Dior heals to complement the dress. As for Murder, he was casual on the high-end, wingtip shoes, slacks, long sleeve shirt, a vest, and a bow tie. The couple fit the part of an amazing pair.

Major was the one to answer the door.

"Barry. How are you doing, buddy?" he greeted. "It's a pleasure to have you two join us." The councilman appeared to have yet again entered into his political element for a moment. "Welcome to my home," he further greeted, then extended his arm to gesture with a wave from left to right. He shook Murders hand, then Charlotte's.

"It's a pleasure to see you again as well, councilman. This is my lovely girlfriend, Charlotte," Murder responded with a bright smile.

"Miss Charlotte. Nice to meet you, ma'am. Barry here speaks highly of you, my dear. He adores you more than you'll ever know," the Councilman now verbally greeted her, as they were let inside.

"Why thank you. And trust me, I know how he feels about us and what we have," she replied, then placed her hand in the center of her cleavage area to display the promise ring he provided her.

"I see you two are moving in the right direction. That's a very good thing," the councilman remarked.

"A very good thing, Charlotte, I assume," Mrs. Appleton greeted. "Welcome to our home, lovely people. We are pleased to have you here for dinner."

"It's a blessing for Charlotte and myself to be afforded the opportunity we now have. It really is," Murder extended his graciousness.

"Please. Right this way," Major said. Then he and Lori led the way to the dining room.

Murder, Charlotte, and the councilman, all took their seats. Mrs. Appleton, made her way back to the kitchen to prepare their meals for serving.

"What type of wine or champagne would you two like?" Lori asked the guests. Our cellar is full of nothing but the best.

"Wine please. Pensfold for me, if you have it," spoke Murder.

"And I'd like your best chardonnay," Charlotte requested.

"Ok. Not a problem. And of course, as discussed, the meal will be steak, baked potatoes, asparagus, and a nice side order of dessert," Lori said.

The day the two were asked to dinner, they'd expressed what they had in mind to eat. Kobe beef sirloins were offered.

Dinner began, and a healthy conversation complemented the occasion.

"So how did the two of you meet?" asked Lori.

Charlotte turned to look towards Murder's direction for him to answer. She had a huge smile on her face. He had no problem relaying their history.

"Charlotte and I met at one of my promotional events. It was hosted at the Eagles Bar, a party to celebrate the Eagles' trip to the playoffs, and a mixtape release of an artist of mine."

"That's awesome, Barry," Lori let out. "I had no knowledge you were a promoter."

"Yes, Mrs. Appleton, I am. Actually, I own an entertainment company, amongst the other business ventures I have."

"That's very impressive, Barry," commented Mrs. Appleton.

"I told you, sweetheart. This guy is going to become a savvy businessman in the near future. Under my mentorship, and with the ambition he has, there ain't no telling how high up the ladder he's going to go," Major chimed in.

"And what about you, Miss Charlotte? What do you do for a living?" Lori asked of her fellow African American sister.

"Actually, I'm in the medical profession, a nursing practitioner," Charlotte made them aware.

"Oh really? Here in Philadelphia?" asked Lori.

"The nation's capital, my current place of residence. And I'm hopeful all may change in due time," Charlotte said, blushing as she looked on at Murder, as she gently stroked him along the cheekbone. His beard had been trimmed low to a 1½.

"That, too, is very good, Mrs. Charlotte. I'm very impressed. You have an amazing display of professionalism about yourself, and cultured in the right way. That's something the both of us have in common as African American women folk. As black women, we strive to make it and enjoy life in the upper crust of society," Lori complimented, in an attempt to plant the seeds of recruitment of Charlotte into her circle.

Lori knew, without a doubt, that if her husband went so far as to welcome anyone into their home, for dinner especially, he had to really take a liking to them and held strong business ties, as well. Lori's agenda was to communicate with the female of any guests, and create a way to benefit from an acquaintance, somehow, along the way.

Lori's eloquent talking points and sentimental compliments was her way of being able to determine Charlotte's level of intellect and whether or not she could match that of her own in speech.

Those etiquette and charm classes Charlotte graduated from benefited her in these moments, a compliment to her professional title as well.

"Well, I thank you, Mrs. Appleton. I'm sure you and I will become real familiar with one another from this evening forward," responded Charlotte, graciously.

"Absolutely. I'd be honored to have that," Lori responded.

They'd completed eating their meals.

"Sweetheart, why won't you show Charlotte around our lovely home while me and Barry go to my man-cave and have a business discussion," the councilman suggested.

"That, we shall do," Lori answered her husband, planted a kiss on his cheekbone, and then stood to go in the direction mentioned.

The women went one way, and the men the other.

Once in the man cave, the two began a game of pool. The real business discussion of the two got going at that point.

"So, I see you've gotten both of these jobs done."

Major was the first to open up. He now had the freedom away from his wife and Charlotte to speak as he wanted.

"I always deliver on my word. My name is Murder on the streets for a reason, nigga. We're in your house, so put all that bullshit political talk right in your back pocket and give it to me raw, like that West Philly nigga you got trapped inside you," stated Murder with a smile. "Four ball going to the left corner pocket there," he called out his shot and pointed with his stick. He had low balls.

Major smiled at him. "You seemed to always be in lock step at every crucial point of the business, aren't you, Barry?"

"Ain't no doubt about it, Mage. I have to be, if I'm looking to get on your level, or higher," Murder replied, expressing his ambitions.

"And I'm looking to teach you how to do just that. You still have a few things to learn, Barry, along with a couple more corners to turn in life."

"Humph, I'm listening. And I'm allowing you the leeway to lead me in the right way. But on another note, what happened to our agreement? You gotta keep your word with me now. I don't want it no other way. You got that?" Murder spat in a tone to clearly indicate how for real he was.

"Again, Barry, our agreement is still in place. It just got complicated, that's all," Major stated.

"Yeah, I know all about complications, a fucking lot. I lost fifteen bricks today, nigga. The very last of everything I had left. So, I'm hoping you still got something? Or your boy C-Ro? Or maybe you two niggaz know somebody?" Murder asked in a demanding way.

"Nah. I'm out of everything myself. And if I don't have nothing, neither does Chandler."

"So, lack of supply ended up being the main reason why the meeting between the distros didn't happen, I assume?"

"Yep, along with the connect being the one to shut everything down. And not just us, the entire U.S. network he has in place has been halted, as well. Again, he went back home to Columbia, to avoid trouble here. It was a move for safety purposes, so to not be arrested," Major made him aware.

"Understood. I get it."

"And I'm curious to know, how did you manage to lose the material you had left?"

"Me talking about it ain't gonna bring that shit back. But if you must know, my stash spot got hit. A thief in the night, so happened to wipe my nose for it. But it's all good. The show must go on."

"A skunk in your cellar? Or someone on the outside?" Major asked.

"Definitely from the outside. My right-hand man lost out on that, too," Murder responded.

"So this occurred today, you say?"

"We found out about it today. It could've happened yesterday."

"And when was the last time you had the chance to check the spot you had the product?"

"That's normally not my duty. I left all that to my right-hand man, Herb. He handles that area."

"And how well did his story check out? Can he really be trusted?" Major asked with a stern voice.

"Look, Major. I know you mean well, and I don't wanna sound harsh when I say this, but I need you to just keep to your end of the deal we got going. Let me worry about how my circle doing, or who could be trusted and all that. And we can continue to be good from there. A'ight." Murder said what he felt needed to be said. He thought it necessary to put dude in his place. But it became too late, in a way, to try and prevent any form of separation between him and his crew that Major's words were subject to cause. The seeds of dissent had already been planted.

"I didn't mean to sound offensive, Barry. I was just saying, only asking general questions, nothing more. But hey, I understand. Let's move forward with our business, shall we?" Major said.

"Yeah, let's do that. Now about my twenty-five grand you owe me, let me have that," Murder demanded his payment.

"I promise you, before you and Charlotte leave, you'll have it in your hands. No doubt about it."

"Good, because I did my part, and I've got mouths to feed and bills to pay. I'm hoping your trip out of the country to go meet so and so will happen sooner rather than later, because the streets are kinda dry right now. Money needs to be made. And you owe it to me and the other distros. The whole network that relies on you," Murder said, making his desires known on exactly what was causing him trouble, atop having his kilos of heroin stolen.

"My trip to meet with so and so, will take place soon. But that's not what the growing concern is at this point."

Murder jarred his head at Major's response. "Well, what it is?" he asked.

"To begin with, so and so had a guy he was close to, probably more so than to me, a Spanish dude. Word is, he had a male along his distribution network, who was killed, a guy by the name Gourdo. And so and so is not looking to let go too easily. Not only that, C-Ro brought it to my attention, along with what I saw on the news, one of his top guys took a few slugs and was killed too, some fella named G-Code," Major made him aware.

"I can't speak to either of the two. I did hear that these two got hit, but I don't know the details, though," Murder responded.

The two continued to discuss the underworld and matters of business. The conversation went in-depth on how they would strengthen the ranks of their own crew, as well as when the supply line would possibly get back rolling again.

Major had fewer problems to deal with or eradicate than Murder did. There were only two people he needed to concern himself with, Murder and C-Ro, but primarily Murder, being that he had too much brewing that may become an issue down the road.

Keeping true to his word, Major paid the 25K owed to Murder before he and Charlotte left his home. The two held mutual business interests. They looked to do more bold acts in the future, possibly additional contract killings. The duo were a councilman and a hitter, the mind and the muscle, a one-two tandem that was looking to raise hell in Philly.

Chapter 7

Murder and Charlotte made it back to the hotel. They undressed from the clothing worn to the dinner and got into something more comfortable. Prior to Charlotte doing so, she needed to relieve herself, the number two. Her digestive system worked very well. She had a regimen in place, where she drank Metamucil three times daily. She went from the toilet to the shower, then into the purple negligee she'd brought along.

Murder was seated on the bed with his back against the head piece. He was pecking away with his thumbs on his phone. Dude had an ass of missed calls, texts and emails that needed to be checked. A personal policy of his was to reply to all contacts that came through his communications devices.

Charlotte sauntered from the bathroom over to the bed. Murder's attention was immediately drawn from the screen of the Samsung Galaxy to the appealing figure of her sexy body there in his eyesight. She stood at the edge of the bed with her hands, palms inward, on her hips and smiling at him, as they locked eyes. He returned with a smile of his own, and then sat his phone on the nightstand.

Charlotte took her phone from her purse, posed for a selfie with the necklace and ring on display, and then played music from her favorite playlist. The tracks were mostly club bangers that had a smooth groove that she could vibe to and be soothed by. She wanted to temporarily transform back to the stripper named Pleasure she once was, the phenomenal crowd pleaser, who knew how to dance her ass off.

Do I post my lovely picture or not? She thought.

Charlotte then eased over to the full length mirror and went into her element. She wanted to put on a show for her boy-toy before finally putting the pussy on him. He was already down to his wife-beater and silk boxers. His hands went down to his manhood. He eased them inside his underwear and grabbed hold of the shaft. Murder then began to slowly stroke himself to bring his Johnson to peak erection.

Charlotte enticed more now, slipping off the gown down to the G-string and nothing more. The beauty of her lady ornaments were on display. Both the nipples had piercings. Her caramel complexion and smooth skin glistened. She had on an exclusive high end body oil that added luster under the lights of the suite. She definitely knew how to manipulate the seductive elements of the given situation.

Well-I-be-damned. She told me once before she used to be a dancer. I didn't know she was this dope, Murder experienced a thought.

Charlotte then untied the G-string and allowed it to fall to the floor. She now only had on the necklace and the ring. They locked eyes again, from the distance she stood. She began to close the space between them, inching towards the bed. She crawled onto the bed, heading up to Murder. Suddenly, she paused midway at his now erect dick at the position of attention through the slit of his drawers. She smiled, then put her focus back on the dick. Charlotte wasted no more time with teasing. The beast in her came out. She went down on him, taking the magic stick into her mouth. The warmth and moisture caused an ecstatic overtaking. Murder's body locked up from the sensation.

"Fuck yeah," he let out.

Charlotte giggled lightly at his outburst, knowing she was doing a good job. As Murder looked on at Charlotte bob up and down on his cannon, with her pretty titties dangling and her exotic fragrance entertaining his nostrils, he had her to pause momentarily, so he could get asshole naked, like she was. They did no talking, only communicating through body language and sex appeal. That was the only dialogue that mattered in that instance.

Charlotte worked him thoroughly with her mouth, getting all sloppy and wet with it. He was almost at the point of climax. She sensed it. Baby girl then backed away, mischievously grinning. She reached over to grab her purse, retrieving a condom, a ribbed Trojan. Charlotte snarled, then ripped the wrapper open with her teeth. She then fitted it onto the head of Murder's cock and rolled it down the shaft completely. Once the protection was properly situated, she then mounted him to do her thing first. Her pretty, clean shaven love box had a healthy color and smell to it.

Charlotte was a creamer. She wanted to allow Murder the chance to witness how thick and gooey she could get with it.

While his manhood was still penetrating her, she spun around to the reverse cowgirl position and began to bounce on the dick, providing him a nice view from behind.

"Ooh, fuck yeah. Bop that ass for me, baby. Do it like you mean it," Murder egged her on.

Whop!

He snacked her on the ass hard. His mood was emphasized in the moment. Charlotte turned to have a look over her left shoulder while continuing to ride the dick passionately, like she was eager to impress him.

"You like this here, don't you?" she teased.

"Motherfuckin right, I do, Sweetie!" he responded. "Why you think I was so quick to put a ring on it."

"So you're mine?" Charlotte asked.

"No doubt. And you're mine. We gonna keep it this way, too. Hopefully for a long time to come," Murder stated.

"You better mean that, too, Barry. I'm so for real, you better," Charlotte declared, then eased up off Murder's gun and lay on her back atop the mattress. She was now ready to have him beat down in the pussy and mean mug her from above.

Murder positioned himself over her in missionary and re-penetrated. He then slow stroked in and out the pussy, looking to work up a rhythm he could flow to, one like Charlotte had going.

Once he'd picked up the pace, his moment of truth was coming on. "Ooh shit, Charlotte. This pussy know it's good to me. I'm about to blow a load, baby," he let out ecstatically.

She looked down in the direction of his dick gliding in and out of her. Basically, being sure the condom was still on. It was.

"Ah yeah," Murder moaned loudly. Then he pulled out of Charlotte, yanked off the rubber and eased upwards to her breast, while jerking on his dick at the same time. He erupted and spilled himself all onto her nipples and belly, releasing everything he had to give.

"Ooh Barry. That's a lot. And it's thick and warm," Charlotte complimented with a smile. Baby girl had already gotten hers off. The condom was evidence of that. It was heavily coated with the froth of her orgasm.

"You put in that work and got down and dirty with it tonight, didn't you, boo?" Charlotte spoke sensuously while giving Murder a pat on the back. He lay atop her, breathing uncontrollably and sweating like a mad man in a crazy house.

He turned to look her in the eyes and smiled.

"You killed it, sweetheart," Charlotte added. "Murder at sixteen hundred Charlotte Ave."

That was a play on the presidential suite they were in and her name, a reference to the actual address of the White House in Washington DC, 1600 Pennsylvania Avenue. She was now the first lady in his world.

Chapter 8

There was a set of elderly white neighbors who lived next to Gourdo's house. They'd began to encounter a horrible odor coming from the direction of the obese Spanish drug dealer. The foul smell caused them terrible bouts of nausea, and they'd even thrown up on many occasions, due to how horrific the smell was.

Gourdo's SUV was taken notice of. It had been parked in the same spot for several weeks, and never moved. This was something that had never taken place at any time in the past year or so he'd lived there.

The original thought of the neighbors was that maybe a pet had gotten caught in one of the water drains and died. But the rain came on three separate occasions, leaving the odor still thick in the air and causing further complications with their breathing. No one could take it any longer. The cops were finally called and a report provided.

The police arrived. They also brought a cadaver K9 unit to assist in the event that death was in proximity. The dog immediately had a hit and led them to the front door of Gourdo's home. The odor intensified the closer they got. The inner windows of the house were swarmed by flies, the filthy ones that landfills draw.

The cops banged on the front door. They got no answer. They then checked the back door. The hitter gained entry through the kitchen window. They didn't immediately discover that it was unlocked.

No further time was wasted. The police broke down the door. Everyone was taken aback by the odor and disgusting sight, which they were ambushed by. There was a large sweat suit clad lump of decaying human flesh, with an outrageous amount of maggots and flies feeding on it. The majority of the six person police crew nearly puked their guts out. A hazmat unit, along with CSI, was called then and there. Based on how the corpse was positioned on the floor, and the details of surrounding things obvious to the naked eye, an apparent cause of death was not readily determined. If homicide was to be the case, motive and evidence would need to be discovered to help them understand what had taken place, and to lead them to a suspect.

A cell phone was collected. There stood the potential of it having a treasure trove of data evidence inside for police. Additionally, in the backroom where Gourdo slept, a cache of military grade firearms, ammo, and four kilos of heroin were found in a hidden location. On the back wall of the closet was a sliding door to where the contraband was stashed.

Due to this high level of material being seized, local authorities had to contact the feds for them to take over the case and begin an investigation of a serious nature.

The identity of the decomposing individual was determined to be that of Tomas Villa aka Gourdo, the leader of the LKNP, and one of the top heroin distributors in the city. And more than likely, the cell phone they now had would provide federal authorities with more than they could bargained for. In their efforts to solve the case, they would get down to the bottom of it all.

* * * *

One week later . . .
The feds now had jurisdiction over the case related to the death of Gourdo. A contact in the cell phone that belonged

to him was to a Felipe Valdez, a name known to them. He was believed to be the supplier of Villa, according to their confidential informant. In further connecting of the dots by the feds, those four kilos of heroin found in Gourdo's home had the same type of wrapping and cartel identity stamp on them as those hundreds seized at the Port of Philadelphia, inside a container. The testing on the material proved that, indeed, they were the same.

Valdez, aka Highway, had fled Philly and headed to California to lay low, being that the heat was beginning to come down behind the investigation of Gourdo's death and the contraband found. He left his brother, Premo, in charge of the operation until he returned.

The feds later learned that a Garrett Culpepper, aka G-Code, had been killed as well. It was discovered that the two, Culpepper and Villa, were connected to the same heroin syndicate. They'd picked up the case to investigate his slaying. They knew he'd been shot multiple times at close range.

The US Attorney office in Philly was faced with a difficult task in trying to track down the leader of a major drug ring by the name of Gustavo Ruiz. He was one of the largest international narcotics traffickers in the world. And according to high level sources, Ruiz would be itching to try to enter the country once more, at some point soon, to deliver more product and to collect the millions of dollars owed to him along the network he provided product.

US Attorney John Fletcher, formed a special task force unit to tackle the growing issues the Ruiz cartel presented. It was dubbed "Operation Ruin Ruiz."

Chapter 9

Dorian Culpepper, aka "Dee Dubbs," the brother of G-Code, was approached by Murder and Herb at the game room he owned down in South Philly. The two were looking to have a discussion with Dee Dubbs, on whether or not he wanted to continue being a part of the distro network with the crew he inherited with the death of his brother.

Following two in-depth conversations Murder had held with Major, he was confident that the supply, would soon flow again soon, and wanted to be sure that everyone was still on board from the black distribution chain of command he had a seat at the table with, and hadn't splintered off, like the Spanish cats were faced with along their line.

Each distro unit suspected the other of foul play somewhere in the mix. And now that Gourdo and G-Code had been murdered and out the way, speculation ran rampant with one side blaming the other. The Spanish dudes didn't know if it was the blacks or other Spanish cats who'd hit Gourdo. And likewise, the blacks didn't know whether or not it was the Spanish cats or other blacks who'd hit G-Code. Not to mention, the fact that the meeting never took place further complicated the matter.

But the audacity and the balls of Murder to step to the man's brother, offering flowers and a business proposal, after being the one to kill dude, was an act, which was out of this world bold.

Murder was the one to open up about all he had in mind to put in place.

"Dee-Dubbs, first and foremost, allow me the opportunity to express my condolences to you and yours over the passing of your brother," he said, then awaited Dubbs to reply. That way, he'd have a good understanding on where his mind lay regarding business.

"To be honest, Murder, I'm not sure if I should accept that from you or reject it, as crazy as shit has been out here in these streets. These vicious streets that is, my nigga," Dee-Dubbs responded.

"What you supposed to mean by that?" Murder had to ask.

"What I mean by that is this. It ain't no sincere niggaz in these streets, not at all, my nigga. I say that because I don't know who it was who got my brother. And I'm not gonna rest until I make shit right for him."

"And I stand with you on that. It's the reason why I'm here to begin with," Murder shot back.

"And exactly how do I know if you are serious or not?"

The way Dee-Dubbs framed the question proved to be an insult to Murder. He felt disrespected in a way. But didn't want to react aggressively, to avoid exposing a degree of guilt in the process.

"Dubbs, if anybody should, it should be you. G-Code was like a brother to me. One I never—"

"But he's not, my nigga. He was my brother. And if that was the case, how you just put it, then why you ain't out here with me, trying to get down to the bottom of this shit?" Dubbs posed a powerful question.

Murder had to pause and think up an answer good enough to appease Dee-Dubbs. He then proceeded. "And who's to say I'm not? I'm out here in these trenches every day, my nigga, keeping an ear to the ground on everything."

"Nigga this Philly! A hitter that was as good as the one who got my brother, definitely won't be out here speaking on it! But I feel strongly that it'll come out some type of way, at some point soon. And me and my niggaz gonna go brazy the moment it does. No doubt. But enough on that. We're gonna handle it. Now, talk to me about the business on your mind. Hopefully, the pipeline has opened back up again with the supply," Dee Dubbs stated.

"Nope. Not quite yet. We working on it, though," Murder declared.

"So how you wanna talk business?" Dee-Dubbs spat. He had a serious tone to his voice.

"I'm just trying to be sure everything lined up and everybody on board, once things get going again," Murder said, referring to the last conversation he and Major went over.

Murder knew he had the edge over Major.

"I think I'll keep my shit moving like I got it, with the old head out in West Philly, Lenny J. It's not as much as it used to be when bro had shit poppin. But it's something. And he supplies it steady," Dubbs informed Murder.

Old head, Lenny J? Murder had a thought over the name. It came to him who dude was. He hadn't heard that name in a long time.

"You say it ain't much but it's steady, huh? But why not keep shit rolling like Code had it going?" Murder asked.

Herb finally spoke up. "I don't know if you know or not, Dubbs, but your brother, G-Code, never broke rank and bought product outside of our chain of command, lil bro."

"That's understood, and I'm aware of that. But the reality of the situation is I don't trust you niggaz. I don't know y'all. And on top of that, y'all niggaz ain't even got no work to satisfy my thoughts to begin trying to trust y'all. So how you niggaz don't expect for me to go about doing business the way I am and find a way to eat?" Dee Dubbs expressed himself.

"Dubbs, look bro. I'mma leave you with this to think over because I've got other business to attend to at the moment as well," Murder let out, once he had dude's full attention.

"Speak your peace," Dee-Dubbs urged.

"Once we get this pipeline back up running, I'll be sure to keep G-Code's seat at the table open, just in case you change your mind and reconsider. We good on that?" Murder wanted to know.

"Let me ask you something, my nigga," Dee Dubbs said.

"What's that?"

"Why you seem to be eager to keep shit moving with the team my brother built and he is not even here no more? I mean, it's not like me, or anybody else, know you like bro did. And you appear to be getting at more, like you trying to get a hand in on something. What that be all about?" Dee-Dubbs asked Murder specifically. He had a smirk on his face as he looked on at Murder. His expression was as if to say he peeped game.

Murder paused again before speaking too fast in offering an answer. He didn't want to run the risk of exposing himself as being the one who'd whacked G-Code on suspecting him of hitting his crew. Also, Murder had ambition to steal away the soldiers G-Code left behind, and the territory that was up for grabs. Who was Dee-Dubbs to stop him? *And who was he to maintain a crew like G-Code had?* Murder thought.

The front running leader of all that was taking place was Black Jermaine. He calculated correctly. He knew that the moment he put into play the motion with Murder, that Murder himself would be the one to begin knocking Power pieces off the chess board of the distro network and go after workers and turf. The hang-up in their plan happened when Dee Dubbs gained control of his brother's operation. Most of the soldiers were now Bloods, like G-Code and Dee-Dubbs were.

Murder and his people had no part of any gangs. He ran a drug enterprise that was free of gang bangers. And now, the

55

only way he would be able to get Dee-Dubbs to see things his way and convince him to continue doing business in the way G-Code had was to produce product. Or soon, if all else failed, he'd simply whack Dee-Dubbs, the same as he had his brother.

Murder finally responded. "That's because, Dubbs, me and Code had a bond like no other. And we made plenty of money together. The whole set up we had with the supplier worked. A lot of product got moved, while the soldiers protected the operation. But an easy way to put it. You got guns and turf, the distro network can continue to benefit with the blueprint that's already in place," Murder explained. His efforts were still not getting any interest from Dee-Dubbs.

"That makes sense. But that was how shit used to be. Somebody killed my brother, my nigga. His blood on their hands. How do I know if or not some motherfucka' in the network you speak so highly about didn't have anything to do with it? Me, personally, I can't trust nobody right now, my nigga, nobody outside of the tight knit Blood circle we got going. So it's best to continue to move on doing shit like I have, doing shit my way," Dee-Dubbs stated emphatically.

This nigga sound like Usher Raymond, Murder thought.

"That's understood, my nigga. I only gave the supplier my word that I'll pay you a courtesy visit because he asked me to. But, you go on and continue to have it *your way,* as you put it, if it suits you," Murder lastly said, then he and Herb went on about their way.

The so-called negotiations with Dee-Dubbs proved to be a failure. The idea Murder had in mind was to have someone else return at a later date, possibly to make him an offer he couldn't refuse.

Murder and Herb continued on to their favorite barber shop—Shear Magic—to get a cut and a beard line-up.

* * * *

At the US Attorney's office in downtown Philly, the head man appointed to run the office, US Attorney John Ramsey Fletcher, called a meeting of all his assistants to discuss the potential take down of the international drug lord Gustavo Ruiz. He had a ten-member lineup of prosecuting helpers. There were six men and four women.

There was this one female from Fletcher's crew—a Spanish sensation—who knew the City of Philly and the streets very well. She was knowledgeable of a lot of the die-hard and dominate figureheads of the underworld. The female AUSA, had grown up with them and went to school alongside them, as well. She wanted to prove herself to be a valuable piece as a prosecutor in taking down the bad guys.

Fletcher opened his meeting.

"Okay, listen up, everyone. Here is what we have and what we know. We're looking to dismantle and then take down the operations of this international drug cartel leader Gustavo Ruiz. He's a Colombian national with a dual citizenship of his home country and the U.S. His drug network has expanded over four of our states, California, Texas, New York and, ironically, here in Pennsylvania. Don't ask me why the Keystone State and not Florida or some other, I don't know. But as you all may know by now, we seized a cargo container that was parked at the Port of Philadelphia. Inside we discovered a large quantity of heroin, pure and deadly, nine hundred kilos to be exact. In addition, we found a dead body resting at the bottom of the river. A few arrests were made. And we managed to convince a couple of Ruiz's workers that it would benefit them more to work with us now, against Ruiz, than to go off to prison for the rest of their lives for him. They made the right decision to cooperate," Fletcher elaborated, then took a pause with his monologue.

He flipped through the pages of his notepad and wrote out something on the board, where he had photos of criminals posted.

He continued, "Here's a diagram breakdown of Ruiz chain of command and the people involved, or once were but now deceased.

Tap!

He placed the yard stick onto the board to point out individuals.

"This here is Mister Gustavo Ruiz, the arrogant, murderous, drug dealing smug, for all he's worth. We now know he has two distributors, whom he delivers his product to, and they sell for him. One is Spanish, a Felipe Valdez, aka Highway. He's the leader of the Latin Nation Dragons, or LND's. They operate primarily in North Philadelphia. Valdez is distro to this guy here."

Tap!

"Here, is a Damon Aguilar. At one point, there were two distros to Valdez with this guy."

Tap!

"And here, is Tomas Villa, aka Gourdo. Someone clipped him days prior to this special clandestine meeting that was supposed to have taken place between the Spanish and black distribution network Ruiz has. He supplies them all. The meeting was canceled at the very last minute according to our CI's and the other sources we have," Fletcher said.

He then went on.

Tap!

"This here is the unknown person, who's one of the three distributors Ruiz deals with personally." There was only a picture of C-Ro, they had no name. "We only know that the enterprise he's a part of, along with another African American Ruiz deals with personally, that makes up the trio, calls it The Council. The other guy, a faceless kingpin, we know not an f-ing thing about, and don't have any leads to help us come to know who he might be," Fletcher informed.

"Isn't that the name of the criminal enterprise ex-drug kingpin Nicki Barnes operated?" asked a black female AUSA.

"Who?" Fletcher replied, having no idea who she referred to.

"Nicki Barnes, a seventies heroin kingpin up in New York City?" AUSA LaChina Smith remarked.

"I have not the slightest clue, Miss Smith, and wouldn't think this to be a continuation of that, due to the era we're in now," responded Fletcher.

"I was merely noting the same name of the two enterprises. That was all," Smith lastly said.

Fletcher proceeded. "Moving along. We have quite a few confidential informants from the African American underworld. I'm confident we could lean on them and press them to help us gain any type of knowledge on . . ."

Tap!

He pointed at a large question mark photo on the board.

"—who Mister unknown here may be. He's the leader of The Council," Fletcher stated.

"Sir, I have a legitimate question I'd like to ask, if I may?"

"AUSA Bryan Harlow?" Fletcher responded.

"To help me better understand it all, how does "question mark" there—head of The Council—relate to the Ruiz investigation?" Harlow asked.

"It's because "question mark" there, who we desperately need to find out who he is, happens to be Ruiz's top black distributor here in our jurisdiction. If we take down Ruiz, so falls he, and likewise, if question mark falls first," Fletcher stated.

"Got you on that, now I'm understanding," Harlow replied humbly.

"So just to clarify things for you all, Ruiz has one top Spanish distributor he supplies and two African American distros. Thankfully, when the decomposing body of Tomas Villa was discovered, along with guns and drugs, his cell phone helped us decipher the network the Spanish dealer had up and going. We were able to make a few arrests, wiretap communication devices, and gain additional C.I.'s.

However, no information came about to help us solve Villa's murder, and we now know the cause of his death. Villa's untimely demise gave us a peep behind the curtain into Ruiz's hand on the Spanish drug trade. Now, if we can only gain that type of advantage into the world of Ruiz's African American distro network, we'll really be in business," Fletcher proclaimed.

A male African American AUSA by the name Gregory Williams chimed in. "So, you mean to tell me that our office doesn't have any leads at all on who Ruiz's top black distro is?" he asked.

"Not one lead, Greg. But what we do know is that there became an issue somewhere along the Chain of Command— trouble in paradise—so to speak, which caused Ruiz to become upset. He was looking to replace somebody upon his visit that got cancelled. We were close to him. Somehow Ruiz got tipped that we were on our way to nab him soon. He stayed away. The U.S. government doesn't have any cooperation with the Colombian government, for many reasons before our time here." He gestured with a wave of his hand at the staff that was present. "Nonetheless, we do know one thing. Gustavo Ruiz, is an extremely arrogant guy. He loves money, probably more than he loves life itself. He's adamant about having a rescheduled meeting with his distro network. That way, he can collect the money owed to him, possibly reestablish a different supply route, and get things back to working as before. Therefore, we've got to throw a monkey wrench in his machine to jam it up. I need you all to find out the time and location of this next meeting the moment it is scheduled. If you have to, beat your C.I.'s out of any information you can to help us come closer to knowing who "question mark" there is, so we can have him and Valdez lead us directly to Ruiz. In other words, follow the money in order to locate our guy, the one and only Gustavo Ruiz. You can bet your ass he'll be showing up to collect his money. Our best chance to get him is when he does," Fletcher declared in his long drawn out additional monologue.

"I believe I may have a small lead that has the potential to become a bigger one," AUSA LaChina Smith stated.

"How so? And how would it tie into any of this?" asked Fletcher.

Smith then cleared her throat and proceeded with what she wanted to relay. "The girlfriend of a now missing C.I. of mine, who's been gone weeks, says that her boyfriend worked in the drug trade, selling heroin for a guy by the name of Barry Murdoch, known on the street as Murder. She also mentioned overhearing a conversation the boyfriend and this Murder fella had, where Murder bragged about his council, or The Council, something to that effect, was about to give him, Murder, a seat at the table, and he'd be provided product again, soon enough, and would be able to increase the amount his workers were supplied. In return, the workers on his team would be making more money than they'd ever made in their life," AUSA LaChina Smith stated.

"This former C.I. of yours, are they on the list of missing persons?" asked Fletcher.

"Yes, sir. They are. I was sure to include them."

"So, it's now safe to make us all aware of who this person is, in the event a connection is made between the confidential informants we have on our own caseloads," Fletcher encouraged.

"Absolutely, sir. My pleasure. His name is Montez Shaw. He went by the nickname 'Duck' on the streets."

Chapter 10

Herbert Glover, or simply "Herb" to family and friends, stood at six foot two, dark in complexion, athletically built, possessed good wavy hair, wore a goatee, and dressed in dope street gear. He received a text message on his personal phone. The number it was from wasn't recognized by him. There was a DC area code. The person who contacted him was someone who wanted Herb's friend Murder to hook her up. It was Imani.

Imani: *Hey. Is this Herb's number?*

Herb: *One of them. Who's asking?*

Imani: *It's me, Imani, the friend of Barry's girl.*

Herb: *Oh yeah. He did mention something to me about you. I've been waiting on you to hit me up. What took you so long, sweetheart?*

Imani: *Well, the wait is over. LOL. I'm about to call now.*

She wasted no more time exchanging texts. The phone call was made then and there.

"Hey," Herb answered.

"Hello," responded Imani.

"Hello," Herb shot back her way playfully.

"Hey." she tagged along in play." How you been?"

"I've been good. I can't complain. Great to be alive, if you ask me," Herb proclaimed.

"Indeed, it is. But I just want you to know I've been checking you out ever since the day, months ago, when me and my girl made our way to Philly and connected with you and Barry. You're a handsome dude, Herb. I must say," Imani expressed.

"Well, I thank you. But you wanna know what's crazy? How about, you remember me, what I look like, and probably everything I had on that day—"

"A nice and fly Gucci suit," Imani cut in.

"You see. And I like that. But I don't really remember you, or what you look like. Not even if my life depended upon it."

"I would video chat with you, but I don't want to spoil the surprise for you. I wanna have a little fun. I can tell you this much, though. I ain't no ugly bitch. I'm thick with it, too. Imani is worth your time and money," she stated with a flare of pure confidence.

"Well damn, Shorty. I think I like you already. You're a confident woman that ain't afraid to speak up for herself, about herself. A man can always come to love your type."

"That's the key word right there, *love*. It conquers all," Imani stated.

"So exactly when do I get to see you?"

It wouldn't be right if Imani didn't offer some type of playful and witty remark.

"You can right now. Just close your eyes, think deeply on how you imagined I looked and put a face and body type to the voice you now hear. And voila, there I am. And once you do that, I want you to hold on to that thought until we finally do meet. Okay," Imani said.

"Mm-hmm. Yeah, I like your sense of humor, too. Keep poppin' your flavor just like that. You gonna mess around and have me hop in that big body Beamer of mine and hit the highway, headed to DC to see you. Keep on enticing me with the conversation."

"Mm. You'll do that for me, Herb?"

"In a heartbeat, and I don't even know you like that. Not to mention, I have no clue how you look either. But I'm pretty sure you're good to go. You're Murder's girl—"

"Murder?!" Imani retorted, taken aback by the name.

"Yeah, Murder, Charlotte's boyfriend."

"I'm so sorry, Herb. But I don't know anybody by that name," Imani stated.

"My bad. I'm sorry. I meant to say Barry," he corrected.

"Now that's more like it. How did he get a name like that anyway?"

"It's just a play on his last name, really. Murdoch. Murder is the rap name we gave him because the nigga known for killing tracks and beats in the studio," Herb explained, the mild version, though.

"Oh. Okay, got you. I understand now. Didn't before, but back to you. About this big body Beamer you speak so fond of."

"Big body Beamer, baby. A seven-sixty, to be exact. A spaceship. You feeling me?" Herb bragged on about his car.

"Well damn. You got it going on like that? What line of work you in?" Imani asked.

"I'm a businessman, period, baby. Entrepreneurship. I own a few thriving ventures. Vending machines, laundromats, car detail shop. Things like that," Herb let her know. "Now what about you? What does Imani do for a living?"

"I'm a registered nurse. Me and Charlotte work at the same hospital. That's how we got to know one another. We've been cool ever since she arrived in DC."

"So are you from DC or not?" Herb asked

"Born and raised, baby," Imani responded.

"And you're what age?"

"I'm thirty-two. One kid. A pet poodle. An ex-husband. And a whole lot of life and goodness ahead of me. What about you?" Imani gave Herb a brief snapshot in words of her current status.

"I'm thirty-four. No kids. Never been married, other than to the game. I take care of family like no other. And I'm truly ready to settle down with someone. Now how did I do?" Herb said, then let out a chuckle at his own wit.

"You spoke well for yourself, Herb. I only hope that you're a spontaneous dude, who has a lot of upside to yourself, and a big dick to keep me right when the time comes and I finally decide to give it to you. And I have to warn you beforehand, this pussy on me is addictive," Imani spat in her savage tone of voice.

"Ooh shit, shorty. You definitely be poppin' it like I like to hear a female pop it, don't you? But look. Check this out, ok. I've got a little business to attend to. You got my number. You now got my attention. And all we gotta do is work to get to the heart of one another. Don't we? Be sure to keep in contact," Herb said. "And good night."

"Ok. And you ain't got to worry about that. I'll be in contact. Good night to you, as well," Imani concluded.

This was the initiation point of a potential relationship between the two, the future appeared to be bright for them.

* * * *

Murder hosted a promotional event at Club Fearless, located on 7th Avenue and Arch Street. The occasion was to bolster the recognition and image of the record label he owned, and to also have two artists signed to him perform a track or two for the crowd. Murder was also in the process of learning the ins and outs of what it was like to be a night life mogul. He held desires to own a club himself someday, or a sports bar. He knew a few dudes from around the city, who'd taken the dirty money they'd made in those vicious streets and invested it into party havens. One in particular, a dapper villain kingpin and property developer by the name "Drip" Savage. He owned The Ozone Bar and Grill, located on 6th and Spring Garden. Murder beheld the same mind set. He envied the Eagles Bar, The Ozone, and Club Fearless.

Dude also wanted to diversify his music vibes, as well, and not be simply limited to the hip hop genre.

The DJ he'd hired for the night knew how to work the ones and twos, as his mix of music, catered to the souls of all ethnicity present in the building. Club Fearless offered a popular and diverse atmosphere.

Murder had his young sensation, Brooklyn, as his company for the night. He wanted to spend time with her, as she'd expressed to him that he'd been neglecting her and his attention wasn't there anymore. Brooklyn took notice of the change he was making. It wasn't like him to all of a sudden switch-up on her and be anything other than who he had been, in regards to what they had.

Honestly, Brooklyn was a very beautiful girl, fit, intelligent and with a desirable dark complexion. She knew what she wanted out of life, and managed to put herself on the path to have the finer things that life had to offer. Murder was lucky to have caught her at a young age. And she'd been hooked on his thug loving from the moment they both agreed to go for it. However, little did Brooklyn know, she had stiff competition in a bombshell cutie named Charlotte. And Charlotte knew her way around the world of seduction far better than Brooklyn did. She'd already scored with a ring and a necklace. This was before she decided to come off the pussy. Not to mention, the level of mental control she held over Murder, as her sex appeal really captivated dude in a way he'd never been moved before.

Murder, Brooklyn and a close friend of hers from New York City, Tiffany, were in VIP. He had a moment to himself to post along the railing of the second-floor balcony. Brooklyn and Tiffany made a trip to the ladies room. He was taking in the surrounding party people that Murdoch Entertainment and Promotions brought out that night. The place was packed, wall to wall, with people from all walks of life, mostly professionals, due to the dress code requirement.

Suddenly, Murder's undivided attention was captured. There appeared this slim and gorgeous Latin female in a cherry red dress and a pair of clear designer label heels to complement the outfit.

He knew, by the cut and style of the dress, it had to be one by Alexander Wang. Dude had bought more than enough of those things to know one by eyesight alone.

Is that Felicia? (pronounced "Fee-lee-cee-yah") He thought over.

Murder furrowed his eyebrows and squinted his eyes to question if it was the sexy Latina he was cued in on.

Oh my. That's her. I know that walk anywhere, and the posture of her body, he thought over once more.

Whosoever the female was, she and a female companion were making their way through the cluster of people, across the floor, to the table section, it appeared to him.

Murder immediately broke from the stationary position he held along the railing and began to speed walk in the direction where the female was located. He made it within arm's reach, then called out to her by a name.

"Felicia. Felicia, is that you?"

He'd gotten her attention. She turned to face him, as the voice kind of gave recognition.

"Felicia. Hey. It's me, Barry," he said ecstatically.

The female then posed a surprised look about her face.

"Oh my God. Barry. How are you? I haven't seen you in years. It's been so long," Felicia responded.

"I know. It really has been. And I've been good. What about you?"

"I've been doing well, Barry. No complaints."

"You still look amazing. Always beautiful as can be," he thoroughly complimented.

"And you still have that charm and handsomeness about yourself that you always had. What are you doing here?" Felicia asked.

"I ah, actually, I'm the promoter of this event tonight. And, the following two Saturdays to come. I'm a night life executive," Murder revealed.

Felicia pursed her lips and leaned backwards with her head in gesture to compliment. Murder then waved his hand along, pointing to the large promotional banners dotted about the club. They highlighted his name boldly, and the company he owned.

"You see, *Murdoch Promotions and Entertainment* . . . that be me, sweetheart," he proudly proclaimed.

"Well ain't this something? Barry Murdoch, an event mogul in the making. You always did have a lot of business about yourself. I'm proud of you," she said to him, then looked at his hand. He was holding his phone. It was the left hand. Felicia was curious to know if he had a wedding band on. Was he a married man or not?

Thank God he's not married, she thought. Neither am I.

"Can I please have your number, Felicia? I'm gonna be sure to not ever lose contact with you again. Ok," Murder said to her.

She called it out as he pecked on his phone with both thumbs to create a contact for her. He then sent a quick text with a heart emoji.

Felicia pulled her phone from her purse, opened the message, and replied with a charming emoji of her own. She then locked his number into her contacts.

"So, who you come here with to enjoy the night?" Murder asked.

"I'm here with my cousin, Jennifer. You remember her, don't you?'

"Of course, I do, ol' Jenny from the block. The one who sings and dances nonstop," Murder responded with humor.

"That be her. She's over by the bar, waiting on me. I don't want to keep her waiting too long. So, I'll call you tomorrow, okay. And it's good to see you again, Barry. I'm sure we have a lot to catch up on," she said.

"We definitely do. And I truly missed you, Felicia. It was good seeing you again, as well. Take care," Murder concluded.

Felicia then went her way. Murder returned back upstairs to V. I. P. where Brooklyn and Tiffany were located. He had a run to make and needed to let her know.

The whole time Murder exchanged pleasantries with Felicia, Brooklyn looked at them. She fumed inwardly at Murder's blatant disregard for her presence there at the club and what they had. But it wasn't so much that he was intentionally trying to disrespect Brooklyn. He wasn't. He just hadn't seen his high school sweetheart and prom queen in many years, twelve years, to be exact.

Felicia Martinez, the Puerto Rican heartthrob, who Murder was crazy in love with throughout their teenage years, had reappeared on the scene after a long hiatus from Philly. At the point of graduating high school, Felicia went off to Loyola University in Illinois and earned a law degree to become an attorney. She made the decision to become a prosecutor. Her career wouldn't have gotten a proper start, had she not done something only two others knew of, God and her sister, Pas.

Felicia, had aborted a pregnancy. Murder was the father, who never came to be. He knew nothing about the termination. She kept it from him, a well-guarded secret, and proceeded on in pursuit of the career she sought.

Two years prior to the night at the club, Felicia transferred from her first post at the U. S. Attorney's office there in Chicago, to the one in her hometown, Philadelphia, PA. Her path as a prosecutor began as a forensic investigator of financial crimes, due to the alarming surge in scam cases the Department of Justice needed to prosecute and dispose of. She then shifted to investigating and prosecuting criminal enterprises. She knew her way around Philly more than the windy city. Also, She had knowledge, to some degree, of the bad guys she'd eventually be investigating and putting away in prison, which helped her make the decision to return home and contribute to cleaning up the community that produced her.

Felicia was amongst the other AUSA's present when John Fletcher gave them the rundown and briefing on Gustavo Ruiz and his operations.

Rather Murder would become aware or not, love and the potential to be prosecuted was the game his fate would have him play. And in this game, one has to win, and one has to lose. There could be no tie.

Chapter 11

The despised uncle of Murder, Dollar Bill, was fortunate to have the opportunity to get back in touch with his twin sister, Karen, the mother of Murder. Dollar Bill made good use of the phone he'd bought from the money the nephew provided. He and Karen loved to talk with one another and reminisce over their days of old, especially about those days of them getting high together and running the streets, doing only God knows what.

On this particular video call, Dollar Bill had a surprise in store for his sister. One he felt confident would sway her to hurry and make it home to Philly for a visit to see him. The two were already deep in conversation when he dropped an atomic bomb on her.

"Karen, how long you plan to keep up that front of yours about not getting high and staying sober and shit? 'Cause you know damn well your black-ass miss the feeling of having that cobra venom shooting through your goddamn veins. Now don't ya?! And they got some shit out here now that'll knock you right on your ass before you even tie up your arm to get it in you," Dollar Bill expressed in his signature humorous way.

He always had the ability to keep people crying and near peeing on themselves in laughter at his witty speeches. It all came naturally to him. He was being himself.

"Dollar Bill. Now you know I've been five years clean now. And I ain't so much as thought about no dope," Karen responded.

"Hell, that's cause you way down there in Maryland and ain't got a nigga like me anywhere on the scene, applying peer pressure on you. That's why!"

Karen laughed like crazy at her brother's remarks.

"Dollar Bill. I don't want nothing to do with no dope. Period."

"Well, why you seem to be so scared to come visit sometime then? That's because you is scared to face your fears, *ha ha ha ha!* Who the hell you think you fooling, gal. I came out the womb four minutes before you did, which means we think alike and got the same type of feelings. I know you better than anybody, Karen. And the same applies for me with you. I'mma be honest with you, okay. I ain't been the same since you been down there, haven't really been able to have fun like I want to. And that goddamn son of yours don't do nothing but treat me like shit. His ass has forgotten I used to change them shitty ass diapers of his, when he didn't know how to wipe his own behind," Dollar Bill expressed. He had emotion in his tone. His feelings were hurt behind how Murder liked to handle him, really fucked up.

"Well, you know how that boy is. He feels like you're the main reason why I began getting high and roaming around out there in those vicious streets of Philly the way I once did. But truthfully, that was something I wanted to do to take the pain away I used to feel emotionally," Karen declared.

Her confession was real.

"Sis. I took care of that problem for you, didn't I? I also went away and did what I had to do behind it, as well. It was no problem for me. That's probably why I miss you so much and want you to come home again. Then we can get back to having some mo' fun, baby," he let out.

He stood to his feet, propped his phone on the table and began to dance for Karen. He had an oldie goldie song playing in the background on his stereo. It was a track by the legendary Al Green.

"I may come to visit sometime soon, Dollar Bill. Can't say when, but soon. And I gotta be sure to keep you and that powerful dope away from me, the stuff you talking about that's floating around now," Karen said, not really realizing that she was on the verge of giving in to those guilty urges she'd suppressed so long. She was interested in hearing Dollar Bill elaborate more about the dope in his humorous way.

"It don't take nothing but a match head of it, you hear me? That shit will sit you on your ass, baby girl. I'm about to do a fix now. Wanna see?"

Dollar Bill was now in the act of trying to coerce his sibling to be a bad girl, along with him. The peer pressure he spoke so openly about became a real thing, then and there, in the moment.

Karen's stomach began to bubble. Her heart rate sped up. Her mouth salivated. She trembled at the legs and hands, and experienced a moment of self-intimacy. She had a premature orgasm, due to now being in a jonesing fit, while watching Dollar Bill fix up, tie up, and then shoot up.

Karen had to hurry and race to the bathroom, lock the door, and turn on the tub faucet to keep her boyfriend, Randle, out of her video and not aware of what was actually going on.

"Dollar Bill. Why you pressuring me like this?! You know I'm trying to keep away from that life now," she said to him.

"And while you find yourself so busy trying to keep away from it, I'm busy trying to gravitate to it. Now ain't that a bitch?"

"You stupid, Dollar Bill," Karen blurted with laughter.

"Hell, I'm just telling you the truth. You see it's one thing I've always been, sis, that's real with myself about who I am and what I do. I'm a user, a dope-head. And once you're a junkie, you'll always be a junkie. That's just the bottom line to it all," Dollar Bill spat before the effects of the heavy *cobra venom* in his vein took over his body.

Karen sat atop the toilet, looking at her brother, not really sure how she was supposed to feel about what he'd stated. Tears streamed down her face. She was emotionally jammed between a rock and a hard spot now. Depression loomed.

Dollar Bill knew her well. He made that known. The sibling also knew that Karen, wanted to continue to be clean and live a sober life. But at the same time, he also knew she missed the world she came from. Deep down, Karen wanted to return to the playground and have more fun, if not but on a temporary basis.

The thing was, there was nothing wrong with a person going out and getting high. If that's what they do, that's their business, so long as they know their limit and don't go too far. This was the area Karen had no control. She abused drugs. It wasn't a habit, but rather an addiction.

Indeed, Dollar Bill didn't want her to return to Philly and end up getting stuck there, or in that life forever, the life of a heroin user. Murder would kill him dead for sure. Dollar Bill only wanted his twin to express herself and do what she felt was necessary to be done, so as to relieve the stress and depression she experienced, in the way she wanted, and with him one last time, before it was all over.

"Karen. You-still-there?" Dollar Bill asked. He was now in a heroin induced stupor and slumped low in a recliner of the apartment he lived in.

"I'm still here, nigga. And your ass high, too." she replied.

Karen then shook her head at the sight of Dollar Bill.

"That must really be some good shit to put a nigga like you down for the count," she joked, referring to the tolerance level Dollar Bill had.

He smiled wildly at her wise crack, revealing his dry mouth and rotting teeth.

"I told you, baby. Only a match head of it, that's all it take."

"I'll be home this weekend. Don't tell anybody. Okay?" Karen let him know.

She'd given in to the whims of the joneses she began to have in the moment. Karen was on the verge of relapsing. Her twin brother was to blame, if she fell weak and went back to the big bad boy, smack. And he wondered why Murder hated him so much.

"I got something very important to tell you, too, when you get here. I only want to do so in person," Dollar Bill made her aware. His voice was drowsy as could be.

"Okay. No worries. I'll be there. Just be easy," she lastly said.

They ended the call at that point.

The issue that caused Karen so much emotional pain and pushed her to begin getting high on heroin was that when she and Dollar Bill were young, about 13 years of age, their mother's boyfriend used to sexually molest her.

When Dollar Bill, whose real name is Kevin, learned of this, he vowed to put a stop to it, and promised to protect Karen from there on out.

One late night, the boyfriend was in a drunken fit. He found his way to Karen's room, as he always had, anytime he felt the need to want to practice his madness upon the little girl. This had been going on for the past year, at least four times a month.

On this particular night, little Kevin caught the boyfriend directly in the diabolical act. He ran back to his room to retrieve the gun he had, a .25 automatic. Kevin then raced back to his sister's room, where the madman was just a humping away atop of Karen.

"Motherfucka'! Get off my sister," Little Kevin yelled out.

The man rolled to one side to turn and look. He'd heard a familiar sound. The pistol was cocked, and a round loaded in the chamber. The guy had a potbelly. Portly. Karen was then able to come from under the smothering position his torso pinned her in.

There was a half-empty liquor bottle within arm's reach, a fifth gin bottle. The boyfriend grabbed hold of it by the long neck.

"You little bastard, what you gonna do?! You need to be happy I ain't fuckin' you, too! You little punk motherfucka, what you gonna do?! Shoot me?! Huh?!" he spat aggressively. He then flinched forward, trying to grab ahold of Kevin with his free hand. That was all she wrote.

Pow! Pow! Pow! Pow! Pow! Pow! Click!

Kevin got off all six rounds the gun had in the clip, the maximum it could hold. He hit dude in the chest, gut, and head. Not one round missed. He then walked over to his sister and helped her put on a different set of clothes, the others were ripped from her body by the now dead rapist.

An elderly neighbor heard the shots and called the cops. The mother of the twins was at work that night, like most nights. She had a job at a nursing home from 11 P.M. to 7 A.M.

When the cops arrived, they found one dead and a set of distraught teen twins. The gun was recovered as Kevin simply dropped it to the floor to go to the aid of his sister. She had an emotional breakdown right then and there. Throughout the entire time the sexual assaults had been going on, Karen was under the threat of death if she revealed anything. That was why she never said anything until building up the courage to say something to Kevin. It was all over from that point. The madman could hurt her no more.

Kevin was arrested, charged and sent to the youth detention center. He ended up doing four years for the gun, not for the killing of the predator. Apparently, the gun had been stolen from a pawn shop that was broken into. Kevin and his buddies were responsible.

Karen, on the other hand, was taken to the hospital that night to be checked and treated for diseases. There was a venereal issue, gonorrhea. She was then taken to a juvenile psych ward for immediate counseling and mental health observation and care.

The traumatizing ordeals Karen was forced to endure lingered upon her for many years afterwards. These became the primary factors, which led her to drug use to help cope. Kevin simply made the choice to do so while in college. He would later begin to rip and run the streets with other drug addict friends. Karen made it her business to join in on the fun, only after graduating high school and having Murder and Quana, her only two.

Part Two

Chapter 12

The texting and verbal phone conversations between Herb and Imani increased. It led to them now being eager as ever to finally meet up in person. Instead of Herb traveling to DC, thirsty after her, she made it her business to hit the highway and head to Philly, alone, to meet up with dude.

The way Imani's train of thought worked, she really wanted to out-do her friend Charlotte and all her Murder had going on.

Healthy competition ain't never hurt anybody, Imani vehemently thought over.

The girlfriend, Charlotte, had really rubbed it in well, bragging about the promise ring and necklace she'd gotten as a gift. Not to mention, the outstanding treatment Charlotte now received at work from Doctor Henderson, and her circle of medical cronies.

On the surface of things, Charlotte was indeed winning. All across the board she was. But the past life she concealed lurked below and held far more ugly things out of the sight of everyone.

Like the friend, Murder, Herb was a die-hard street nigga, but, had a sure touch of class and sophistication to go along with it. He wanted to treat Imani to something not too high class and not too beneath her. Something ordinary couples could appreciate, then later, get to the extraordinary things they'd worked hard together to enjoy. A meal and a movie, nothing too exotic, Red Robin's for now.

Herb texted her the address and directions to his spot. He had a low key pad in North Philly, not too far from I-95, on Lehigh Avenue, close to the exit ramp. The GPS system helped her make it to the destination. The time was 5 P.M on a Thursday. Imani was high energy and needed no rest.

The Red Robin's Herb had in mind was located outside the city. He held a psychological fear that someone possibly was eager to take aim at him, to rob, kidnap, or to potentially, kill him, behind past bad deeds. Security was his reason for wanting to dine elsewhere. He took that more seriously than anything. Not to mention, they both loved this brand-new restaurant. He knew of a Red Robin's in the next county up, Bucks County, heading towards Doylestown. The two hopped in Herb's big body BMW 760 IL that he spoke so highly about to her, the *spaceship*, and were out.

An interesting conversation sparked between the two throughout the drive.

"So, am I all you imagined I would be?" Herb asked. He had a bright smile about his face.

"Oh you definitely are. I couldn't wait to lay my eyes on you. That's why I was eager to get here. And I love your hair cut and beard line-up. It's dope," Imani complimented, stroking his ego.

He took a glance over at her, smiling like *Prince Hakim* on "Coming to America," showing those nice white teeth of his and feeling superior about himself behind the compliment from the cutie in his ride. Imani was really feeling him too.

"I thank you on that. I really do," he responded, then reached over and gently stroked her along the cheekbone with the tips of his fingers.

Her honey complexioned skin was soft and smooth to the touch.

They arrived at the restaurant, got out, looked one another over from head to toe to observe how well dressed they were, and then held hands. Herb planted a kiss on her forehead. Imani smiled in pleasure.

Like before, he was draped in an outfit he knew she would admire and desired to see him in once more. Herb donned a freshly bought Gucci sweat suit, the fleece sports type. He also had on a pair high top Gucci sneakers to complement the look.

Imani wore a form fitting dress, black in color, that had wide straps to it, which crossed the breasts and tied behind the neck. The back was open, revealing more skin. Baby girl was fine as all outdoors. She presented a lot of sex appeal, very provocative and alluring. Herb had himself a winner.

Once inside the eatery, they took their seats, ordered food, and got back to the conversation that they were already holding. They wanted burgers and fries.

"So Herb. You work for, Barry? Are you two business partners, or are y'all two longtime friends who just happen to have it going on together?" Imani asked of him.

"We more the last one you mentioned. Been cool many years, since we was about ten. It used to be three of us, me, Barry, and a cool ass white boy named DJ, Douglas Johnston. As we got older and in the streets, along came a dude a few years our senior, named Jermaine, Jermaine Styles. DJ moved away though. And Jermaine ended up in prison. But yeah, me and Barry are just two street raised hustlers who so happen to be making it in the City of Philly our own way," Herb replied.

"So this hustler mentality you mentioned. It is out of habit, or out of necessity?" She posed a powerful question.

Herb smiled at her. He then offered a response. "That's a good one there, never thought about it in that way. Why do I hustle? I guess it's safe to say I love to hustle. I love the grind. I love the streets. And this is who I am. But I'm currently in my transition phase at the moment. I'm trying to legitimize it all. I'm glad you asked because I wanted to explain myself to you in person, and not over the phone.

Hopefully, you can understand where I'm coming from on that. My reality won't come into conflict with how you see me, nor into what we may be looking to establish. I know it's best to be real with you," Herb laid out in a sincere tone of voice.

"You're good. Don't worry about a thing. I'm here with you, ain't I? I made it my business to leave DC and drive nearly five hours to your city to go out with you. And I plan to stay overnight, maybe the whole weekend. We shall see. Let's just continue to enjoy one another and be aroused by our chemistry. Ok," Imani stated with excitement. Her smile was electrifying. Her seduction compelled him to return one of his own.

"You're so dope, Imani. I really like your personality and your style. This is meant to be. Ain't no way I can go out and fuck this up. I don't think," he responded with a light chuckle. He was shocked to think he'd say something like that about himself.

"Who's to say? It may just be. I'm willing to put in the work, though. All I ask is that you continue to prove me right. Don't make me out to be a fool. And don't let me down in the least. Me, and my daughter, and our pet poodle, would greatly appreciate it if you turn out to be the man in my life that I've always desired. My ex failed us badly."

"Damn. That's weak on his behalf."

Imani's phone rang. "Herb, may I take this? It's my boo, Charlotte," Imani asked politely.

"Sure. Go ahead."

"Hello," she answered.

"Hey, 'Mani. How are you doing?" Charlotte responded.

"I'm good. I am good. I'm out right now."

"Oh, you are? I hear the excitement in your voice."

"Yes, girl, I am. And I'm loving it, too," Imani declared while looking across the table to smile at Herb.

"And just who is the lucky guy to cause you all this joy? I haven't heard you like this in a while."

"Well, if you *must know,"* Imani now switched to her *Downtown Abby* British accented voice that she and Charlotte took on in character and play.

"I'm out with Herb right now, down in Philly," she revealed.

"Oh. Is that right? I'm glad to know that it's all working out. I'm very happy to know this," Charlotte responded in character play as well.

"Me too," Imani let out happily.

"Well, you two go right on ahead and enjoy your date. And I want all the details, too, bitch, when you make it your business to cross that line. Okay," Charlotte said, as she smiled into the camera on the phone.

Imani had her Bluetooth earpiece in. Herb knew nothing that Charlotte said to her.

"If anybody, you know you'll be the one to get it all when the time comes. Now I'm gone. Take care, baby," Imani said.

"You, too, boo," replied Charlotte.

The call came to an end.

"But yes, Herb. Where were we?"

"The ex of yours," he reminded.

"Oh yeah. That part. As I mentioned before, I was once a married woman. Happily so, for the first two years, and then everything went to hell. He's the father of my daughter. Her name is Farrah."

"So what happened?" he asked.

"Long story short, he failed to man up. He was selfish. He became controlling, and wanted everything his way, but didn't pay the cost to be the boss. I found myself doing more for us than him. And he had a good paying job, a construction worker, a certified brick mason," Imani revealed.

"But I don't understand. How could y'all go wrong? With him being a brick mason and you a nurse?"

"It's because before me, he had two other women he has a child by. He pays heavy child support for them both. At the time, I hadn't made RN status yet, only a CNA. I wasn't making the type of money I do now."

"This sounds like a dude you may have had a crush on in school then finally was able to have him later in life," Herb stated his assumption.

"How are you so spot-on like that?" she let out with a smile.

"I just am. But let me guess, if I may. Dude was a star athlete in school? What sport?"

"Basketball. How were you able to put all that together, Herb? I gotta know."

"It's because I'm a man myself, Imani. That one was easy to figure out. A guy with three baby-mommas and a selfish attitude, like you describe, had to have gotten a lot of attention at some point, and was probably slinging dick like it was no tomorrow."

"He definitely was doing that! But, in the end, it wasn't worth the problems I was put through with him. It turned out to be an ultimatum of either good dick and misery, or no dick and happiness. I think I made the right choice by choosing the latter," Imani stated.

"So what, you just been going with no sex?"

"Yep. I got caught up with my career and my daughter. I do have a vibrator, though. He hits the spot like I want him to all the time. His name is *Bob*. We're locked in like that, too," Imani playfully let out.

"*Bob* the *boner*, huh?!" Herb blurted with a laugh. "Well, hopefully, I'll have the opportunity to put Bob's ass back in his place, for good."

"You just may, tonight perhaps. You talk a good game. And I'm hoping that will carry over to you having a good game to back it up. Judging by the print in those sweat pants you got on, you just may live up to the hype," Imani responded, then went on to have a thoughtful moment to herself, a strong fantasy.

The two completed their meals, then made their way to catch a movie. They went to the theater connected to the Franklin Mills Mall in northeast Philly.

The time was still early for a Thursday, only 9:00 pm. Imani already communicated to Herb that her plan was to keep him company all throughout the night, or the weekend even. If all continued to work out in the way that it was, she'd pack a bag for a three-day occasion. Herb convinced her more and more of all the reasons why it would be a good idea to continue to entertain one another. Things were going well.

Chapter 13

Imani and Herb made their way to the popular South Street strip to stroll along the sidewalk and have a look inside the many shopping stores that lined the strip. The conversation continued between them.

"So, Herb, be straight up with me about something, okay? Because I'm sure there are. But I simply got to ask, so you can't later say I didn't know."

"I'm listening. What's up?"

"How many other females you got?" Imani asked, as they walked and held hands.

"I'mma be honest. I'm not gonna lie to you because I'm aware it's best to let it all out in the beginning phases. No doubt, I've got a jumpoff or two I fuck with every now and then, but only when I get those urges to want to have sex. However, as far as me having a main lady, nah. And if I did, you think I'd let you leave your car at my place the way I did? Not hardly. That motherfucka probably would've been destroyed by now," Herb responded with a laugh.

Imani had to laugh herself at his remark.

Damn. He does make a strong point. If he had a girlfriend, why would he allow me to leave my car at his place? That wouldn't make any sense. It'll be crazy. And messy, Imani thought to herself.

"So you got two jump-offs you bang every now and then, huh? I believe I have what it takes for you to focus on only one. Me. Because I'm damn sure not gonna put myself in the category of simply being a jump-off, one you bang when you want. And yes, I'm willing to give it a try, we're gonna have to learn how to practice being monogamous, Herb. Okay."

"*Monogamous.* Big word for me there, huh?" Herb responded.

"Big word for big people. Serious inquiries only, baby. It's on you," she fired back. A loving smile appeared about her face.

Herb continuously took glances at Imani from her head to her feet. Her sexy figure caused him to smile and lust over her. Along with the fact that she chose him, he was convinced, thus far, that Imani may be the top female for him, no other. And she wasn't even from Philly. This made the situation better.

They locked eyes and exchanged smiles. Herb then gently squeezed her hand. This was to signal to her that she'd made the right choice. He was leaning towards accepting her proposal.

Once the two left South Street with their shopping bags in tow, they made their way to a hotel suite at the Comfort Inn over near the airport. The two were grown about how they felt for one another in the moment, as well as about their desires and what they wanted to do. They were ready to fuck, she more so than him. But was Imani willing to give it so fast? Maybe she was, maybe she wasn't, only time would tell.

Imani came out of her dress and made her way to the bathroom to take a quick shower. She exited the washroom wrapped in a towel. Her breasts, hips, and ass bulged under the soft cotton garment. A steady enticement was created. Herb sat atop the bed and was tuned into a TV show the moment his attention was stolen.

Imani eased the towel open to show off the goods as she sashayed from the door of the bathroom to the edge of the bed. She grabbed hold of her phone and put on a smooth music playlist for them to relax to. Ms. Mary J. Blige was her favorite. A track from her *Share My World* album began to set the mood.

Imani now allowed the towel to drop to the floor. She was ass-naked. She locked eyes with Herb, smiling elegantly prior to speaking.

"You like what you see?" she teased.

"Do I ever! Absolutely, baby!" he responded, he now had a sensuousness to his tone.

"Well then, I'm waiting for you to act like it."

Herb leap from the bed to the floor, wrapped his arms around her waist to palm her ass cheeks, and began to ravish her with wet kisses. He was already down to his tank top and boxers. Imani wanted to see how lean and in shape his physique was. She helped him out of his shirt. He was in good shape. Dude loved to work out and box. After all, Philly is known as fight town USA.

"Very nice body you have here, Herb. It really is," Imani complimented. She then caressed him on his chest muscles.

"Yours too," he offered in return, then leaned inward and tickled her nipples with the tip of his tongue.

The two then began to tongue kiss wildly. He had a continued hold on those plump ass cheeks of hers. Herb instantly fell in love with the feeling of her tender buttocks firmly at his fingertips. His touch was stimulating to her.

Whop!

He smacked her on the right ass cheek.

Then the left.

"Ooh!" she cooed. "That felt so goddamn good to me," Imani pleasantly let out. "It's always nice to have a man around to attend to the feminine needs of a woman."

Herb's manhood was erect and stood out through the slit of his boxers. Imani gripped it with her hand and began to gently tug on it until it reached its peak. Dude was built like that, too. He was blessed with nine inches to work with.

Imani took a seat on the edge of the bed. She still had a grip around the shaft of Herb's dick. She then took the head into her mouth and slid those luscious full lips of hers down as far as she could. He shook in reaction to the sensation he felt. Her mouth was warm and comforting.

"Damn this feels good," he let out, and tilted his head to the back, looking up toward the ceiling, and held his mouth wide.

Imani did a deep throat and held in position for as long as she could, then withdrew to catch her breath. Herb's dick was now coated with thick saliva. She loved to do her thing in this area, *sloppy toppy*. Baby-girl wasted no more time. She went to work.

Herb placed his hands on his hips and leaned back. He caused his dick to stretch to the max. Imani continued to handle her business like the undercover freak that she was. Her performance was a combination of bobbing, jerking and working with no hands, at times. Herb reached the mountain top. He was now ready to blow.

"Imani, I'm about to cum, baby," he said to her.

His pistol then began to spit thick globs of his load from the tip. She guided his aim in the direction of her neck and breasts. Nothing entered her mouth or touched her face.

"You do pretty good, Herbie. I can get used to this. Now go on and power up, so I can suck you off more. Then, I'mma let Bob get a little play time in this threesome we got going on here," Imani expressed sensuously, with a smile.

She then walked over to her purse, cum still on her neck and titties, and pulled out the purple vibrator she had. It was about the size of an average eggplant.

Imani had no intentions to give Herb the pussy the entire time they were to be together, only good dick sucks for their first weekend together. He was cool with that.

Chapter 14

Murder took a ride from his penthouse to his father's home in Germantown. He wanted to see how his old man had been doing. He hadn't had the chance to do so in a while. Dude had been too preoccupied with the street life and all he had going on in that regard. His brother, Jabari, the cop, was there, as well. Even they hadn't seen one another physically in weeks, only talked and texted over the phone. There was a need for them to meet up and have a thorough conversation about the undying situation that was going on with the supplier, Ruiz, and, the delay with the product.

In appearance, Murder and Jabari's personal style were totally opposite. Jabari wore a crew-cut, mid-top fade, was clean shaven, and had a pencil thin mustache. His skin complexion was a shade darker, and he was about an inch shorter in height. He also had a more pointed nose and darker piercing eyes.

Jabari, the good son, held plenty of military experience. He'd been deployed to Iraq and Afghanistan on more than one occasion. He served 15 years in the Army. And upon being granted an honorable discharge, he became a cop for the Philadelphia Police Department.

The two brothers greeted one another upon Murder's arrival.

"'Bari! What's good, bro?! How you been? Man, am I glad to see you," Murder let out.

"Ah, man, lil bro, what's been good with you? I've been well. Just living life, you know. Taking things day by day. With the line of work I'm in, you never know what's in store," Jabari responded. His voice was somewhat deep and baritone, but had a hoarseness to it this day, like many before. The years of calling cadences and conducting marching drilling ceremonies in the Army, caused this.

"I've been doing the same on my end, bro, taking things one day at a time. But hey, we need to chop it up with one another before we part ways again. A'ight."

"Yeah. We can do that. We're due for a conversation anyway."

They then walked to the den area where their dad sat watching a baseball game. It was the month of April. The season hadn't long got going. The Philadelphia Phillies played the New York Mets. It was an early season division game.

Jacob Muhammad, formerly known as Jacob Murdoch, was the 64 year old father of the three. There was Jabari, Barry and Ishmael, in that order. The baby boy was only 25 years of age. Jacob had a son by three different women. However, he and Ishmael's mother were still married and together. Her name was Nora.

Jacob and his wife, were members of the Nation of Islam. Jacob's path to being righteous was a complicated one, due to the interference of the street he once was a part of, many years back. He'd served 10 years in prison. Ishmael himself was currently doing time for drug possession. He was sentenced to 84 months federal. Five had been served. Jacob and Nora met through the brother of hers who was also a NOI Muslim. He and Jacob had always been cool.

"What's good, Pop. How you been?" Murder greeted.

"I been good, son. Your dad been well. I'm glad to have you both stop by to check in on me," the father replied. "It's been a while now."

"Yeah, I know, Pop. I've been caught up with a lot of things on my plate lately. And you know my lifestyle. I can't bring that around you, out of an abundance of respect, you know," Murder said to his father in a way he'd clearly understood him and the point he was making. He continued. "I don't want to push my luck and have big bro here to be forced to lock my black you know what up," he said.

The three of them share a laugh at Murder's remark.

"Seems to me, you know how to handle your business. You haven't gotten locked up yet. My hope is that you got an exit plan in place, son. That's all," the father expressed his wishes.

"I've got one in place. I'm currently making a transition, as we speak."

"Doing what?" asked the father.

"I'm an entertainment promoter, Pop, a night life mogul. I host parties and other events. I have a recording studio, too. The name of my company is *Murdoch Entertainment and Promotions.* The name you and my mother gave to me when y'all brought me into this world," Murder stated.

"Speaking of your mother, How she been? Haven't seen her in a while either," Jacob said.

"Oh, mom been doing really good. Me and Quana paid her a visit not too long ago."

"That's good. She still in Maryland?"

"Yep. Her and ol' Randle doing real good."

"Well, that's so good to know. I'm just glad to have my boys here to see me today. The baby-boy should be free soon too," Jacob informed.

"How much time Izzy have left?" Jabari asked.

"Not long. Maybe a year. He's been down five now."

At that point, Murder pulled out his phone and made a few clicks on the screen of it. Apparently, his actions had something to do with his young brother. He felt the need to do something for him.

"Bam! I just put a few dollars on Izzy's account. He should be good for a little while now," Murder declared. He put $1000 towards Ishmael's commissary.

"Well, I'm sure he's glad to have a strong family support base. He definitely has that," the father stated.

Jabari then pulled out some money and handed to the father to provide the brother with. He gave $500.

The visit to Jacob by his two sons went on a little longer. Then it was time for the two brothers to have a discussion they were looking to conduct. They hopped in Jabari's SUV and began to tour the city.

"So what's on your mind? What you wanted to speak with me about, my brother?" Jabari initiated.

"Yeah, bro. I would've been called, but I've had too much crazy shit going on in my camp. I really wanted to speak with you on the business me and your guy, Appleton, got going on," responded Murder.

"What about Major? He's been doing the right thing with the business, hasn't he?" asked Jabari. "I'm sure, no matter what, he gonna keep it real on his end. And I see you took care of that business for him, too, on both ends.

"Damn. He mentioned that to you?" Murder responded.

"Bro, *I'm* the one who got him all the information on dude and the girl. And I'm the one who linked the two of you together to begin with. You must've forgot about that or something?! I saw it on the news, too," Jabari brought to his brother's attention. Not to mention, I know you and how you get down. I'm your brother, nigga. My plan for the both of us is bigger than you may know."

"So Major reports back to you on things, I see!" Murder had no clue of all the moves his brother was making behind the scenes. He was completely oblivious.

"Look, Barry, I'm gonna go ahead and let you in on what the business really is, because I see you honestly don't know. And this appears to be the right time now. You're in deep enough at this point."

"Please do, nigga, because I'm so lost," Murder declared. Jabari chuckled at his remark.

"Listen, bro, I'm the main reason Major was able to connect with the supplier the way he has."

"Say what?!" Murder asked in surprise.

"Yep. No Gustavo Ruiz, if no me. You and he are both only pieces on the board to the greater scheme of things that's currently playing out."

Murder had a thought. So the plug's name is Gustavo, I see. I'mma be sure to mention that name to Major at some point, to see what type of reaction I get from him.

"I'm bigger than you may think, bro. The men of the world with true power, who really call the shots, are unknown and are never seen nor heard from by those not at the top," Jabari stated.

"Tell me more about you being one of the power players behind it all, since the time is now right." Murder was eager to know more.

"Why you think I served all those years in the Army, nigga? Then later became a cop? Never mind. Look. I'mma give you the story. Okay, remember a few years back, when Obama was President, a scandal broke out about members of the CIA and high ranking officials of the Army getting caught up in a whore house down in Colombia, partying with prostitutes?"

"Man, you know I wasn't up on the news like that back then, but I think I recall catching a little bit of it. Anyway, what the fuck happened?" Murder urged Jabari to get to the meat and bread of the story.

"Well. I was first lieutenant of a unit at the time. It was us who was there. The Captain of the unit and I, came across the opportunity to meet Gustavo then. The occasion at the brothel was actually thrown by the cartel leader himself, to create a smokescreen to hide what was really going on."

"And exactly what was that, bro?"

"There were heavy deals between the Cartel Chiefs, guerrilla rebel leaders, and the US Military for guns, ammo, fuel and an unquestioned level of protection. All that was in exchange for narcotics and undisturbed access to the natural resource mines down in the country," Jabari relayed. "The rebels, cartel leaders, and, the local tribe people, lived in the area of the mines. The government was looking to gain total control of the region and not do right by the people who lived in the area, so, a civil war ensued."

"So the cartels, rebels and tribe leaders was at war with the government?" Murder asked.

"Right. Led by a corrupt president of theirs. Someone they hated. Obama was supposed to have held some kind of peace summit negotiations there in Colombia at the time. Basically, a bunch of political mumbo jumbo to hide what was going on. Not long after that, Obama goes to Cuba to meet with Raul Castro. Then, the embargo was lifted, and America and Cuba resumed doing business once again. Obama made dual agreements with two Spanish speaking countries. But back to Colombia."

"—Yeah! That's what I wanna know more about," Murder stated swiftly. "Gustavo and Colombia, bro."

"My captain and I, a guy who spoke Spanish, himself, had direct access to Gustavo at his processing plant, located in the jungle. It wasn't too far away from one of those mines that they needed our guns and muscle to protect. They also needed our fuel to operate the machines used to extract the material from those mines. Gustavo, had a whole lot of product, but, no place to sell it. Then, when the agreement between America and Cuba went through, there wasn't anything in our path to stop us. The product made its way up the east coast, bypassing Miami and all the heat associated with its ports and the guards there, and, being delivered instead, to the ports of Philly and New York city respectively," Jabari elaborated on for his brother, a rare thing. He broke it down to help Murder understand better.

95

THESE VICIOUS STREETS 2 | PRINCE A. TAUHID

Basically, he went through a lot of shit to get to where he was, and, there was no room for fuck ups.

Jabari continued. "America needed the lithium from those mines to put in batteries the electric vehicles took. Companies were beginning to explore manufacturing electric vehicles during this time. That's basically what America was down there for, to help bring an end to the civil war, offer a solution, and capitalize in the process. And if all failed, simply take the resource mines for ourselves, the true American military way," Jabari said with a smile.

"Now how did Major become a part of all this? I missed that part," Murder stated.

"He was somebody I was familiar with who moved weight on the low, a lot of it. And Gustavo only wanted three people from Philly to deal with. My captain knew one, a Spanish cat they call Highway, and I knew one, Major. I had him pick the third person, someone he knew he could work hand in hand with."

"And he's Major's right-hand man, C-Ro?" Murder asked for confirmation

"Exactly! And through it all, I get a certain percentage of everything Major and C-Ro make in the process. And my former captain do so with his people."

"Goddamn, nigga! You making all the power moves behind my back, with me included, and I ain't know shit about it," Murder blurted out with a smile.

"It wasn't for you to know, at least not at the time. But hey, I'm letting you know now."

"But I'm curious to know, bro, why did you get out of the military, only to become a cop, when you can be in the position that Major's in?" Murder felt the need to ask.

"It's because, lil bro, I'm busy gaining more power through the ranks of law enforcement than I would have by being a civilian. I'm not focused on getting money and being rich. *Power,* is what I really want. And why put myself out there and expose things when, in all actuality, I don't have

96

to. It's not necessary. I let Major do all he do and I get my cut. And the moment his ass begins to feel himself a little too much, then I've got two ways to get him. One; I can send so and so; and two, I could send my brothers in blue at my behest," Jabari declared in response.

Murder looked at his brother as if he were an evil genius, a mad scientist even, of the most epic proportion. He commented. "Nigga! You got this shit all figured out, don't you? Smart motherfucka you. How long you been planning this shit, Bari?"

"Ever since the moment I had the opportunity to meet Gustavo Ruiz, bro. I took strong advantage of it. And you know what?"

"What's that, bro?"

"The best part about it all is that you're the one and only person I ever told the story to, no one else. Major doesn't even know. And you're not gonna say a fucking thing to him about it either. I need you to simply keep doing things the way you are, and everything gonna be alright. A'ight?" Jabari ordered.

"No doubt, bro, I got you on that. But I've got to at least know, to satisfy my own curiosity, why did the nigga Major want those two jobs done that I took care of for him?" Murder asked.

"The dude, Errol, tried to go too far. He was attempting to extort Major out of his seat as a city council member. He'd threatened to expose some of the things he knew Major had going on behind the scenes. That would have triggered a strong investigation, which in return could've compromised the entire operation. And the female, let's just say Major got himself in a little trouble with his dick. That's the best way to describe the situation. It wouldn't have been a good look to have a sex scandal involving a councilman blazing across the headlines of the media. And also, she didn't want to have the abortion he told her to go through with, nor sign the nondisclosure agreement and take the hush money he tried to provide. So as a result of the bitch being stubborn and hard to deal with, she became collateral damage. What more could we say or do? We tried. But she played hard ball. We had to whack her," Jabari explained.

"So Major lied to me then, about the girl," Murder stated

Jabari shrugged his shoulders. "He probably felt it was best that you not know the full details. Either way, they both had to go."

"Yeah. Maybe that was best, huh?"

"Yeah, didn't make any mistakes, bro. Everybody is covered. There hasn't been any kind of blow back. No repercussions to worry over."

"Okay. Bet. But what's up with this Gustavo dude? When he plan to open the pipeline back up? The streets is starving out here for that dope. We need to feed 'em."

"That's not my area, bro. I left that to Major. It's not my area," Jabari stated with emphasis.

"But you do still have contact with Ruiz, don't you?" Murder pushed it. "We need product."

"Yeah. I do. But like I just told you, that's Major's area. I'm out the way on that. There's not a need for me to contact Ruiz. I linked him and Major, then stepped back," Jabari reiterated.

"Bro, look, I gotta ask you this here, too, right. Out of all the people you know of in the streets moving weight and doing their thing, why you overlook me and link Major to the connect? You know, without a doubt, you was supposed to have offered me the first opportunity to work directly with him," Murder expressed.

"And why was I supposed to have done that, again?! Because you're my brother?! That's why you feel the way you do? What makes you more qualified than Major? What type of network you got that's more established than his? What type of people in your corner, other than me, to back you up? But before you offer to respond . . . Nigga! Let me help you understand a thing or two about this shit, if I may.

Major is an elected city council member. Upstanding tax paying people put him in power. That means . . . he's got the whole city of Philly backing him. Judges, the DA, the mayor, every powerful person in this town, especially from the democratic voting party. You got that kind of pull? Fuck no! I would've been a damn fool to not link a nigga like him to a connect I lucked up on. You're just a street nigga, bro, who can be thumped out the way at any time. You don't have that type of power and influence like the nigga Major do. And that's why I overlooked you for him, it just simply made more sense to do so. Besides, I wanted you to be the enforcer on the streets, the muscle backing Major. That's why I put you two together."

Jabari was sure to provide a detailed explanation to the questions his brother asked. He continued to speak further.

"But cheer up, nigga. You still on the team. You getting money. And you're eating good. You're the number three in line on my team. And not only that, Major paid you a hundred thousand to put down two bodies. I could've had him go out to get another nigga to do the job, who probably would've wiped out all of north Philly for that type of money, like Pol Pot did to his own Cambodian people. But I didn't. I had him to tap you, because I knew you'd go for it, and do the job well," Jabari said, then paused to see what Murder's reaction would be.

He then spoke more. "Bro, look, I've got to continue to do my part, and that's not so easy. I have to be the person I have been, the *poltergeist* behind it all—"

"The who, nigga?!" Murder cut in to ask.

"The poltergeist, nigga! That means, the ghost behind the scenes making all the noise and moving all the pieces. An unknown boss. The power player," Jabari clarified.

"And what you looking to achieve out of all this?"

"Well, my plan is to move on up to the Homicide Division, at some point, then run for office as a municipal politician. A magistrate judge, a city councilman, like Major, maybe a run at trying to be the mayor, or possibly go for governor of Pennsylvania. I've got a thirteen year plan in place. That's why I keep my hands clean the way I do," stated Jabari.

Murder thought over again. This nigga really got this shit figured all the way out, don't he? Bro the man behind it all, isn't he? A very discreet guy. And knows how to move properly.

Murder really had no clue of how deep things were that he was involved in. And now, if things got sour between him and Major, he wouldn't be able to touch him, not without his brother's permission. No matter how bad things got, Major was the number one business partner to his brother, and they both worked for him.

There was no doubt about it, Jabari Murdoch was a major figure in Philly's streets. Team Jabari, Major and Murder, yeah that's them. They had it going on.

Chapter 15

Quana and her boyfriend, Heeme, began to hustle and get money together, as they never had. The two had stepped up a notch from the small supply, Heeme once provided, to a larger quantity he now was working with. Those 15 bricks of heroin he stole from Murder and Herb came in handy. The lick was on time. And the boyfriend-girlfriend duo was clocking dollars, like no other.

Heeme had a place to live of his own now, something Quana hated with a passion. This was because she could no longer control him the way she once had, when he was between her place and his mom's. Also, Heeme was a hot topic to all the thirsty females, who wanted to put the pussy on him, but no one wanted to go through the bullshit they knew Quana would come with, if she found out. That could be a serious thing, death even.

The two sold weight, ounces or more, at a time, nothing less. And with 15 kilos to work with, there was a lot of product to get rid of. Heeme had to play it smart. He knew everyone was aware that Quana was the sister of Murder, so his plan was to play the role that best worked for him, acting as if Quana was the one behind it all. She went along with his plan, and didn't question it once.

Heeme only put out so much of the product at a time, to keep people from becoming suspicious and having word get back, through the streets, to Murder and Herb that Quana and Heeme had work. But at the same time, the streets also knew that Heeme was the brother of another heavy hustler, JJ, and they both were the sons of Charlie Jones, the elder brother and JBM leader of Aaron Jones. However, the Jones bloodline sold a different product. Coke.

Heeme hadn't too long returned to his place from a trip he'd taken to the suburbs, Bristol, Pennsylvania. He had a few cats up that way who bought his material. Quana was there. They were up, counting money.

Since the time he'd stolen the heroin, he and Quana had sold six kilos. He had been slow rolling at a steady pace. *Easy does it*, was his philosophy.

"Ninety-five . . . ninety-six thousand . . . ninety-seven thousand . . . ninety-eight thousand . . . ninety-nine thousand . . . one hunnid K!" Declared Quana. "Baby, we at a hun-dun and going!"

She was excited as ever to have something to do with the type of money they had at their hands.

"We at a hunnid so far, huh? On our way to the top, baby," Heeme responded with a smile and fist full of cash that he'd counted himself. A rubber band was placed on each $1,000 stack.

Heeme leaned over to kiss Quana. He slithered his tongue in and out of her mouth. She loved it when he gave her that type of attention.

"Motherfuckin' right, we are. It's me and you, baby. Only me and you," Quana said, awaiting him to at least offer some type of reply in agreement. He didn't. Why did he do that?

"You hear what I said, Heeme? It's me and you, right?" Quana repeated her words. She now had her eyes locked in on his. Her mouth was wide, and a look of anxiety came across her face. The bitch was crazy about Heeme.

To her chagrin, he still didn't say anything in response. Dude only smirked, stood to his feet, and walked over to place the cash into the shoe box in the closet.

Quana jolted from the top of the bed and gave chase in his footsteps. She was now up in his face.

"So you don't wanna answer me?! I said, it's you and me on our way to the top, isn't it?!"

"Quana, why you busy tryna start shit with me? How you gonna ask a stupid ass question like that and you see what the fuck the obvious answer is! Ain't no other female here helping me count out a hunnid fuckin thousand dollars, and selling this goddamn dope, now is it?! So what the fuck does that mean?! It means, it's the both of us, don't it?! What the fuck?!" Heeme got loud on her, loud enough to where the neighbors of the apartment could possibly hear him vent.

"I only asked you a simple fucking question, Heeme. And all this could've been avoided."

"Yeah, by you not asking the fucking obvious," he cut her words short. "But why you trying to start something? And where all this attitude coming from?"

Rather Quana or Heeme had any idea, Quana may have been battling with a case of borderline Personality Disorder. She alternated in and out quite often. And her attitude put people off about her, except those who were already used to it, and knew how to deal with it.

Quana went on to reply to the question asked of her by Heeme. "It's because I'm pissed off at you for not answering your phone when I called. That's why," she said to him.

"Man, get the fuck outta here with that shit, Quana. That was damn near two weeks ago. And I told you, I had to make a run. I was driving with product on me and didn't need to be disturbed, not by you or by no one. A'ight," he ranted off a few words, hoping that she'd let it go.

"I just don't want to lose you, Heeme. You're all I got, as far as somebody to love, and somebody knowing how to handle me. That's all," Quana confessed.

"Quana. Honestly, if you keep up this type of shit, you gonna push me away from you. Ain't no nigga got time to be going through no shit like this, when there are other options that'll bring peace and move chaos out the way." Heeme kept it real with her.

"I'm sorry. I apologize for how I acted," she said, attempting to make amends. But the damage she'd already done to the relationship thus far had already been too much. "I don't trust well, Heeme, and you know this."

* * * *

Two Weeks Ago . . .
Heeme treated Quana and Tatiana to a day out. They went to the laser tag play center, then to Dave and Busters. Even while out with her boyfriend and cousin, who was like the sister she never had, Quana was so jealous over Heeme. She refused to let him out if her eyesight. And when forced to do so by something he needed to do alone, she would repeatedly call his phone to keep a check on him. Now that Heeme was making a couple of dollars, and was a rising star in the dope game, this intensified how she felt, and made things worse, being that he had a fleet of females ready to hop right on his dick the very second he had the opportunity to get out of Quana's eyesight.

While at D and B, seated at the table, enjoying appetizers, Heeme toyed around on his phone. He had a female cousin doing time in the feds who wrote dope urban fiction books. He had a designer create a few book trailers for her and he promoted. Heeme was already trying to get into the independent filming industry with the money he was checking in, and developed a following on social media, mainly on Instagram.

"Well damn. My IG at Heeme-the-film-mogul is poppin today, I see. We going in," he boasted, referring to the large number of comments and views coming in from the three trailers he promoted.

He'd said it loud enough so Tatiana could hear him loud and clear. She was on the team now, and helped Quana sell her portion of the product she had the responsibility to get rid of, the same way Quana helped her kill somebody.

The two females held that much trust in one another, and nothing or no one could break that bond or come between them. No one, except maybe a handsome dude who was in good shape, getting money like crazy, and had a fierce dick game that could satisfy even the biggest nymph. If only he could avoid the girlfriend he had and sneak away with another chick to get his freak on.

Ever since Quana began bringing Tati around Heeme, the two would lock eyes and share a smile at any opportunity they had, anytime Quana looked away. Tati and Heeme never were provided enough time to exchange phone numbers to entertain the dangerous game that they wanted to play, at least not until this day D and B's.

At the time when Heeme blurted out his IG tag, Tatiana knew that was cue for her to memorize it for a later time. Her intuition as a woman who was determined to have her turn with a man she was infatuated with motivated her to this conclusion.

When Quana and Heeme dropped Tati off at home that day at an apartment over in West Philly, which she lived in alone, they hadn't even made it back across the bridge over the Schuylkill River before Tati was already in dude's DM, leaving a message. She had a good idea that Heeme dared not allow Quana access into his phone, no matter how hard she tried, so Tati was in the clear to shoot her best shot. She wanted him to herself.

When they finally made it back to Quana's place, she was in a rush to use the bathroom. Those spicy ass wings, sauces, and fries had done a number on her guts, and she needed to take a crap to regain a level of comfort again. This became Heeme's chance to check the message and reply.

Tati: What's poppin, pretty boy? Please tell me your phone secured.

Heeme: Always. Ain't no jawn got that type of power over me.

Tati: Good, because you already know how that crazy bitch is about you. Hell, the way she brag about you and what y'all got going on, she made me definitely wanna know what the forbidden eggplant hit like.

Heeme: Mmm-hmm. You wild shorty. You know that?

Tati: Mm-hmm. Not wild as I wanna get on that lethal dick I know you got on you.

Heeme: How bad you want it? Lol.

Tati: Just as bad as you wanna give it to me. And you know you do. (Smiley face with the tongue sticking out)

Heeme: So what you wanna do first, suck or fuck?

Tati: the other four letter word, both. LOL. (Another smiley face emoji with the tongue sticking out.)

Heeme: SMHWS. I definitely want it now. And I'mma pull on that long hair of yours, too, while I fuck you hard from the back. So your pretty mixed ass better be ready for this dick I got for you. Ok.

Tati: ooh! Savagery I see. I like that. Lol.

Heeme: Hey, gotta go. I'll be there in an hour to pick you up.

Tati: Can't wait (in my NY Jets Bart Scott voice), lol.

Quana came out and took notice of Heeme at the kitchen table weighing up some of his heroin product on a digital scale. She'd taken a quick shower while in the bathroom, as well, and was now in her forest green bra and panty set. Her smooth dark skin glistened from the baby oil she had on.

Quana walked closely to Heeme and then kissed him, rubbing on his arm at the same time. He had on a wife beater.

Whop!

He smacked her on those plump ass cheeks as a response to the kiss and caress of his muscles.

"What you got going on, sweetie?" Quana asked him.

"I've gotta go take care of a couple orders. Everybody called while we were out and about," he replied. Telling half the truth.

Damn. This nigga gotta go back out again tonight I see, Quana thought to herself.

"Okay. No problem. Just handle your business and hurry back to me please. I've got something you need to attend to. And this kitty of mine purring like crazy to be stroked and pounded," Quana said. "So I'll be waiting."

She kissed him once more, then turned and made her way to the bedroom, tossing her hips really extra from side to side, as she activated her sensual mode.

Truth be, Heeme actually had a few drops to make, in addition to now having Tatiana on the to-do list. He took up thirty more minutes of time putting the packages of dope together then prepared to make the drive up I-95 to the suburban city of Bristol, Pennsylvania. He needed to stop by his spot, too, in South Philly, to drop off cash. Also, he needed to check on the remaining kilos of product he had left, to be sure no one had crept behind him and stolen the material he'd stolen himself. Now how ironic is that? A thief afraid of another thief. A guilty conscious would never allow one to rest properly.

When he made it to his spot, he had $20k to stow away. He then headed to west Philly to scoop up Tatiana. He sent a message voice to text to her while driving. He let her know he was on the way.

Tatiana replied by telling him she would be at the door waiting on him to pull up.

Shortly thereafter, Heeme was there, Tati hurried from the front door and hopped into the car. Initially, the two didn't say anything to one another, they simply locked eyes and smiled. The feeling and thrill of it all stimulated them that much more.

Suddenly, Tati rushed him from the passenger seat. They kiss wildly, like they were two long lost lovers who hadn't seen one another since middle school. A pause occurred, so they could catch their breath.

"What took you so long to let me know you wanted to fuck with me?" Heeme asked.

"Shit, nigga. I ain't know how to get in touch with you. That crazy bitch won't allow you no room to do shit, not even to breathe. That was a smart move you pulled, though," Tati replied, then smiled and kissed those pinkish lips of his once more. Her infatuation with him showed more. Tati then pinched his beard at the chin area. He had a thick, full one.

"We ain't got to rush. We got time," he made her aware.

"So, where we going?"

"I gotta make a stop or two up in Bucks County. After that, we'll get a room up there. Then I can finally know what that pussy of yours hit like. You feel me?" Heeme let out with a huge smile.

"Mmm. Fine by me. How much time we got together?"

"As much time as I want." He uttered with a chuckle. "Quana must really got the boo-game down on you, from what I see," he joked.

"Nah. I just know how crazy that bitch can get about you. That's all," she responded.

Heeme then pulled off.

Chapter 16

Once Heeme and Tatiana made it to Bristol, he made a stop at his guy Lonzo's pad. He had a spot in the village, a small community, not far from the highway. He served dude the ounces he wanted. They then left, headed down State Road 413 towards the Burlington-Bristol Bridge. Heeme turned left onto Route 13, the direction that led towards Trenton, New Jersey. There were many hotels lined up along the way. He and Tati stopped at the Quality Inn and checked into room number 269.

From the moment they entered and closed the door, Tati was on him. The two hurried and got out of their clothes, continuing to hug and kiss.

"If only you knew how bad I've been wanting this," Tati said to him.

"And if you only knew how bad I've been ready to give this dick to your ass, you wouldn't believe it," he responded promptly.

Tati dropped to her knees on the thick carpeted floor and took Heeme's dick into her mouth. He was near peak erection already and now had all the reasons in the world to reach the max potential his manhood was capable of. He had a nice size to him. She smiled and stuck out her tongue upon first look at what he had to work with.

She gripped both hands tightly around the shaft and bobbed on the head in rapid fashion. She then did a deep throat, came off momentarily for air, then did it again. Tati tightened her suction with her jaws and lips and jerked him off while gliding those saliva coated lips of hers down and back along his oversized shaft. She had good timing. Here sensor indicated to her he was on the verge of blowing a load. She wasn't ready for him to do so, not just yet. Although, he was built to go back-to-back.

Baby girl eased off him and stood to her feet. Tatiana had one amazing body, maybe due to her mixed genetic background. Her naturally long, black, curly hair flowed past her shoulders. Those honeydew melon sized breasts sat up nicely. And her thighs were plump and toned.

She smiled at Heeme as they maintained strong eye contact. He leaned in and took her left titty into his mouth. She loved the feeling that sneaking and creeping with Heeme gave her. It was some type of natural high she'd never experienced.

"Come on," she uttered, then turned to face in the opposition direction, putting her back to him.

Tati leaned over onto the bed. She licked the four fingers of her right hand and glazed her love box with her own saliva.

Whop!

He playfully smacked her thick yellow ass. A rosy, red color appeared as her natural feminine musk invaded his nostrils. He turned into a wild dog on the loose with a hard dick and a pair of hard nuts.

Neither one of them had any condoms and didn't seem to care.

"Heeme, I want you to fuck me really good from the back and pull on my hair while doing so, like you said you was going to do. Okay," she motivated him with her freaky speech.

The head of his dick was already at the entrance of her honey hole by the time she completed her sentence. He penetrated, then began to thrust with a slow passionate flow to his rhythm. The dick was now fully inside.

"Ooh yeah. Ah. Fuck me. Fuck me good. Just like this," Tati moaned and panted ecstatically.

Heeme leaned over and nibbled on her ear.

"You like this? Huh? Tell me you do. Say my name while doing so," he said in exhale.

"Ooh yes, Heeme. I love this. Fuck me. Go faster," she egged him on.

He did what he was told. He grabbed a fist full of her hair, wrapped it around his hand, and pulled passive aggressively.

All of a sudden, Heems's phone began to vibrate on the table, in an out if control type way, like it was a combination of calls, text messages, voice mails, and email alerts. He had a good idea of exactly who it was and why they were calling. Quana. Trying to force him back to her faster. The calls didn't stop. And neither did he. Dude was too preoccupied stroking in and out of a really good shot of pussy raw-dog, with a female he'd instantly taken a liking to.

Heeme was now at the point of climax. Tatiana had already did her thing. She heavy coated his dick with the sweet cream of her candy box. From the head of it all the way down to his pelvic, the evidence of how pleased she was showed.

He slowly pulled out. His cannon blew. The thick gooey release plastered the crack between both her ass cheeks. She loved the warmth and the nasty feeling of his load oozing down the line.

"Ooh shit, Tati. Fuck yeah. Damn, that felt good," Heeme let out in pleasure.

"Yes it did. Yes the fuck it did," she cosigned his words.

His phone began to vibrate once more. Tatiana didn't have that type of problem. She'd turned her phone off altogether. And more likely than not, no doubt, Quana had tried to contact her, as well, to vent about something possibly, only for her calls to go directly to the voicemail system. Now Quana had to really be pissed. There was one hell of a coincidence there she had on her hand. Her

111

boyfriend wasn't answering his phone for whatever reason he felt he didn't have to for her. And also, her female cousin wasn't either.

What the fuck was really going on? A scenario Quana could question.

In the meantime, the sex was so good to both of them that neither Heeme nor Tatiana wanted such a sensational escapade to come to an end so quickly, at least not yet.

"So what now?" Tatiana asked. "Since we've started something, we may as well embrace it all the way."

"What you mean, *what now?*" Heeme retorted with a smile. "We bout to fuck some more. Then again. And again. And we may stay together all night. This what you wanted, ain't it?"

"Hell yeah. I'm playing a dangerous game to get it, ain't I? So I may as well go ahead and drain you dry, while I got you here with me. We can worry about everything else later down the line. Now come on. Let me get that dick back rock hard again so you can bang my back out doggy style, just the way I like it," Tatiana encouraged.

She sat on the edge of the bed atop a towel and began to suck on his dick once more. They were so into one another that not a moment was allowed to be wasted, not even to take a quick shower. Time was of the essence.

* * * *

Meanwhile . . .

Quana fumed vehemently behind the fact that Heeme wasn't answering his phone and Tatiana had hers off. Not to mention, three hours had passed since he'd left the house, and he was only supposed to have been gone no more than an hour.

A vicious voice from her subconscious spoke to her. Evil insinuations persuaded.

I know motherfuckin' well those two bitches ain't trying to play footsie on me, right under my nose. I'mma kill 'em both if I find out they are. I swear to GOD, I am. She thought.

There was a serious problem brewing, and no doubt, hell to pay.

Quana hopped up from the bed, dressed, and got into her car. She was headed back to West Philly to her cousin, Tatiana's apartment. She wanted to have a word with her, in person now, about what her and Heeme was going through, if she was there.

Unfortunately, when Quana arrived, Tatiana wasn't home. A bad sign. What was to come next?

Chapter 17

Presently . . .

Quana and Heeme continued to talk as they counted money to be put away.

"Did you hear me on that, Heeme? I said I don't trust well. And I'm sure you know that by now."

"So in other words, you don't trust me? That's what you saying?" Heeme countered.

"That goes for anybody. I have serious trust issues."

"Yeah. You do. And I understand that, but you are not venting this to nobody else. You are doing it to me. So, it has to be an issue you have with me, about me.

"Okay. Since you wanna go there, then fine, Heeme. I don't trust you like that no more. Your attitude and behavior changed on me somewhere along the way. And that caused me to feel the way I now do," Quana revealed.

"And why do you think that's so? The change in my attitude and behavior? It has everything to do with your attitude and the fucked up way you've been behaving, Quana."

"I just told you, I've got trust issues and I don't trust you like that no more. I need to know I can trust you again," Quana said, then paused for his response.

Heeme only looked at her. He said nothing.

"I need to be assured that we got each other's back, no matter what. How do we get to that level?"

114

He knew Quana better than she thought. There was something serious on her heart, troubling her. And he needed to know what, being that he had a sexual affair on-going behind her back with the cousin. He had to do what was necessary to keep that private, if he wanted to live.

"You got something you wanna tell me that I don't know nothing about, Quana?" He asked.

"I may do. Just in case some major shit go down and something happens to me," Quana put out there.

Heeme then provided his undivided attention as they sat atop of the bed.

"What you got on your mind? You can trust me," he asked bluntly. "Huh? What's up?"

"I killed somebody Heeme," Quana reluctant made him aware. "My third body."

Heeme jarred his head in absolute shock at what she'd told him. He knew by the way she said it that there was a lot of truth to it. There damn sure was.

"Hey-hey-hey. Wait a fuckin' minute now. Whoa. What the fuck you mean you killed somebody?" Heeme retorted. "And why the fuck are you telling me this, Quana?"

"Because, Heeme. That last one really fucking with my conscience, you know. And I honestly don't know if I made the right decision to do it."

"Was it you by yourself? What was it a hit and run, or something?" he dug in with his inquiry.

"No," Quana said somberly. "It was me and Tatiana."

"It was you and your cousin, huh."

"Yeah. Me and her."

"So what the fuck happened? Y'all two jumped a bitch or something and she died? What?"

"No. Actually. We lured a female into a house and beat her to death with a bat." Quana gave specifics.

"What the fuck? For what?"

"Tati claimed my brother paid her to do it. But I believe that was a lie. My belief is that the pregnant female we beat to death was probably fucking Tati's boyfriend and he messed around and got the girl pregnant. The reason I say that is because how the bitch Tati been gone all the time away with her boyfriend, then all of a sudden pop back on the scene here in Philly, broke, busted, and the whole nine yards and talking about her and dude broke up? Then, not long after, we go to a bitch's house, and we kill her. It ain't no coincidence that Tati knew where the bitch lived and everything. Now what that sound like to you?" Quana inquired.

"That sounds like a line up with the way you put it," Heeme instigated. "And what the fuck y'all do with the bat and the body?"

"Shit, we left the body in the house where it lay. And I gave Tati the bat. She was supposed to get rid of it."

"So you was the one who did all the work?"

"Yep."

"And now you don't even know if Tati got rid of the bat or not, do you?

"Nope, and now I'm beginning to get scared."

"It's a little too fuckin' late in the game to get scared now. And you say that was your third body? As you put it," he retorted.

A long pause took place. Quana then spoke more.

"It's an ugly reality I now live, Heeme. And you too. Because your girlfriend, me, happens to be a chocolate cutie, who is also a killer," Quana capped. "My brother's name is Murder. We put in work, Heeme, me and bro, and now, the both of us are in it together. You and Me. So your ass may as well get used to it. Because you not going nowhere. And I'm not going nowhere. And I stand on that with my life. On GOD, I do," Quana spat emphatically.

If for whatever reason he wasn't afraid of her before, he damn sure was now. He had good reason to be.

This bitch is really crazy, Heeme thought to himself.

"Well look. Now is not the time to be talking about all that. Okay? I need to be sure and keep my focus. Just don't mention anything to nobody else. A'ight. Words of advice there," he cautioned her.

Heeme now had more problems to deal with, between the street and Quana, than he could ask for. Shit was becoming too much for him to deal with, entirely too much. Mostly from her.

Chapter 18

Charlotte was home alone on this particular day. It was the middle of the workday and she didn't have to return to work for the next two days. Her daughter was away at school. Charlotte had the house all to herself. For a few hours, she slept. Then she spent her personal time binge-watching one of her favorite TV shows, *Claws*.

The series was set in Miami, a place Charlotte was very familiar with. The show brought back many memories. She experienced a powerful moment of nostalgia, so much so that she was compelled to do something she hadn't done in all the years of being away in the Witness Protection Program.

In going against the warnings and orders of the supervisors and handlers of the program, Charlotte grabbed hold of her phone from the nightstand, blocked out the number, and then dialed one particular phone number that hadn't changed in years. It was to Ms. Phillis Margaux, Charlotte's mother. She remained living in Trinidad and Tobago.

Having uncertainty of who the caller was from a restricted number, the mother reluctantly answered anyway.

"This is the Margaux residence," Ms. Phillis stated. "Margaux family residence here. Anyone there?" Ms. Phillis repeated.

Charlotte remained silent. She then began to cry. The voice of her mother caused her to be overcome by emotion.

The sobbing followed. It didn't take the mother long at all to figure out who it was on the opposite end of the line. She knew it was her eldest daughter.

"Carmen," mother dearest called out. "Carmen, talk to me child. What took you so long to call?"

Charlotte sniffled. She then blew her nose with a Kleenex taken from the box that sat atop her dresser. She finally spoke. "I couldn't call you, momma. I was told not to contact no one, for safety reasons, they said," she announced.

"Carmen. How you gonna be in danger from your own damn momma, girl? I don't give a damn what those people say. You came from me. You're my daughter. There's no one who know and understand you better than I do. And what makes you deprive me from my granddaughter the way that you have? My first grandchild?"

"Momma. If only you knew what all I've been through before and after Vershon's trial."

"I'll know soon enough because you're gonna come home some day in the near future and tell me all about it. And I'm not asking either. I'm telling you. I'm your mother."

"I don't know if that's possible, momma. Besides, I don't even have the same name anymore," Charlotte made her mother aware.

"What you mean you don't have even have the same name anymore? That's ridiculous. I don't know but one name I placed on your birth certificate, and that's Carmen Janine Margaux. My first born, by the way. Where are you and my granddaughter now? And what's the new name you so-called have?"

"I can't disclose that in…"

"Carmen," Ms. Phillis cut her off mid-sentence. "I don't want to hear that. Not now. Not tomorrow. Not Ever. You hear me, girl?" the mother verbally scowled.

"Yes. I hear you, Momma," Charlotte complied. "I'm legally known as Charlotte now. Charlotte Thorpe. We live in Washington, DC. I'm a nurse now, at a hospital here, an

NP. There, now you have it. I trust that you'll keep all this to yourself, please. Me and Asia's life depend upon it that you do."

"And what about my granddaughter? Were you forced to change her name too?"

"No ma'am. I didn't have to change hers. I'm just thankful of the fact that the government didn't take her from me and put her through the foster care system."

"Carmen, your mother simply has to know, how did you end up in this ugly predicament to begin with? Please inform me."

"Momma. It's a long story that I really wish not to relive again, if I don't have to. Please don't make me. However, I will say this. That no good niece of yours, Misty, is at the middle of it all. She's one of the main reasons behind the madness."

"I did hear rumors, but I never heard your side. Just give me the gist of it please."

"Misty started sleeping with my man, Momma. Her and Vershon had a sexual affair. That led to me and him going back and forth. Vershon used to beat on me badly. He shot and killed Ralo right there in front of me. And eventually, he got arrested, with the government pressuring me to testify against him," Charlotte briefly relayed.

"So that's how it all got started? Behind Misty? I would've thought Vershon was better than that, but apparently not."

"No, he wasn't. And I though the same, but I was wrong."

"Well, he is a man, and those are some of the things men do. It happens."

"Yeah. You don't say. I had to learn like this."

"So Vershon may be the daddy of that little boy Misty got, too, huh?" Ms. Phillis asked.

Charlotte knew nothing about any of this. She became infuriated behind the mention of it. "What?" Charlotte blurted. "Misty had a baby? A son, at that?"

Charlotte always desired a son by Reign Man, in addition to their daughter. This was so because she adored his physique, his level of intelligence, and the deep degree of love she had for him at the time, in the beginning phases of their relationship. Reign Man had good genes.

"Yes, she did. The boy is about three years younger than Ni'Asia," her mother informed her.

"Oh my God. I remember now. I happened to get a good look at her and the bulge of the belly she had while Vershon's pre-trial motion hearings were taking place. I saw a few pictures of her, too. But, momma, how could my own flesh and blood do me like that? It's not right. It's because of her that everything went to hell."

"I know, baby, I know. But no matter what, you have to find forgiveness in your heart. It's only right that you do," the mother expressed. "It's only right that you do, sugar. That's the best advice mother can give you on the situation between you and Misty."

At the utterance of the word "sugar," a memory was triggered with Charlotte. It was the thought of her best friend Shug. Charlotte missed her dearly. They had a lot of good years together. "Momma, when was the last time you heard anything from my friend, Shug?"

"My black baby, Shug? Sherniece? I haven't heard from her since I last heard from you, many years ago. It seems like forever in a way. She did call when Vershon was found guilty. Sherniece was mad at you, but told me she was still my black baby, and let me know she'd keep in touch."

"You still have that number she called you from?"

"I do. It's wrote down in my contact book I've got in there. Why? Do I need to speak to her for you?"

"Yes, ma'am. That'll be nice. And hopefully she and I could meet with one another there in Trinidad, when I decide to visit. Then we can talk about everything."

"I can do that, and hopefully, she's gotten over being angry at you and won't be so stubborn to not want to meet with you here, at my place."

"I hope not, either, Momma. I miss my old life, my family and my friends. Me and Ni'Asia had to start all over again."

"So that's a yes, you and my granddaughter will be down here soon?"

"Yes, Momma. We'll be down that way soon. I would let you speak to her, but she's in school at the moment. I'll be sure to call you later today and let you talk with her," Charlotte said.

"Please do, Carmen. Momma needed this."

"I understand, Momma. I'm about to go for now. I love you, okay."

"I love you, too, baby. Stay strong and keep in mind everything is gonna work itself out. Okay."

"Yes, ma'am. Talk later," Charlotte lastly said then ended the call.

While talking with her mother, Charlotte received another call. It was from her new friend, the wife of the councilman, Lori. Charlotte wasn't able to take the call while engaged in another. Her intent was to do so after the fact. She returned Lori's call.

"Hello, Lori Appleton here," she answered.

"Hey, Lori. Charlotte here. I see I missed your call."

"Yes. Charlotte. How you been? I figured I'd best begin putting your number to use. Being that you did give it to me personally, while we enjoyed dinner."

"I've been good, Lori. And again, I really appreciate the time we had at your home. Barry and I could get used to occasions like that," Charlotte responded, now putting up her professional persona.

"My husband and I could do the same, as well. It's definitely not often that he welcomes others over. And that's a clear indication to me that he and Barry have a business bond that runs deep," Lori stated.

THESE VICIOUS STREETS 2 | PRINCE A. TAUHID

"I'm sure they do. And as far as you and I are concerned, I believe I can learn a lot from you. Your friendship and mentoring is very much needed by a young African American aspiring woman like myself. And I'd like to know what's required of me to become part of the sisterhood you're a member of?"

Charlotte didn't feel the need to hold back. She got directly to the point of what was on her mind. It was communicated to the powerful councilman's wife.

"Oh, Charlotte. I'm flattered about the uncanny compliments and disposition you have presented, I don't know what to say. You're pretty observant. You have good insight. That's a quality not too many possess."

"That's one of my gifts. Having the ability to properly read people, I tend to get it right more often than not."

"Well, you nailed it. Your assessment of me is a correct one. I'm a woman of influence, my dear. I belong to a strong, committed sisterhood here in Philadelphia, and we are open for recruits. It's one of the reasons I called to offer you the opportunity to apply," Lori stated.

"And I will have to report in person to do so, correct?" Charlotte asked.

"Yes. That is the beginning part of the process, to report in person to apply. I'll be the one recruited and endorsing you, Miss Charlotte, so the process shouldn't be so strenuous. Only one obstacle I see," Lori pointed out.

"And that is?"

"You would have to be a resident of Philadelphia for the time being. It would require you to move from DC to here. And judging from the nice gift your beau, Barry, blessed you with on your finger, the transition shouldn't be a hardship. It seems to me, you two are moving along just fine. There's great chemistry."

"I would have to move to Philly to be a member, huh?"

"Yes, to be within jurisdiction of the chapter here," Lori confirmed. "And I'm sure once the transaction is initiated,

I'll be able to get you on at one of the highly respected medical centers that your title mandates. You've worked hard to acquire your status. There's no going back once you make it to that point, only forward."

"I'd be honored to have you do that for me. But please, allow me the time to speak with Barry first, and also, one of my colleagues here in DC, whom I revere. Once I do that, I'll get back to you, Mrs. Appleton," Charlotte explained her intentions.

"That'll be perfectly fine by me, Charlotte. I look forward to hearing back from you in the near future."

"Absolutely. You take care and continue to be blessed."

"You do the same dear," Lori lastly responded.

The call concluded.

The contact by Lori to Charlotte was something she'd looked forward to from time they first met. Lori's stature as a woman and the influence she held was the type of quality Charlotte secretly envied, in all goodness, though. If moving to the City of Brotherly Love was all she had to do, then she would make a promise to her friends and colleagues, Imani, Mrs. Henderson, and April, that she'd keep in contact often and visit when she could. However, that wouldn't be all Charlotte would need to do. Due to being active in the Witness Protection Program, there would be a necessity for a request to transfer, and consultation, for safety and security reasons. Charlotte had it in mind to contact the appropriate personnel later in the week to get advice.

Being that things began so well for Imani and Herb, Charlotte had it in mind to persuade Imani to follow her lead and make the move, as well, if she decided to so herself. There were options to be contemplated. They'd began to come up at the time Lori mentioned the requirements to her of how to become a part of the sisterhood.

Charlotte was beginning to make progress in the direction she'd long desired. Her life was gradually evolving into one full of prosperity and acquired class, status and taste. Even so, after previously being on the verge of being locked away for life in federal prison or either killed by the psycho ex-boyfriend, Reign Man Aikens.

Charlotte felt blessed, if only she could get back some level of her life, pre-Witness Protection Program.

Chapter 19

Karen was now back in Philly. She'd ended the long hiatus away, down in Maryland. She took the train, got off at 30th Street station, and then a taxi from there straight to her brother's bar-top apartment in north.

Ever since Dollar Bill's daughter made her return, she'd helped him maintain financially. Tatiana paid his rent, light and gas bills, and also cell phone bill each month. What more could he ask? Dollar Bill was able to support his dope habit by detailing cars for a guy who owned a shop nearby. Also, he would clean and sweep the bar he lived over. And if needed, he assisted his drug supplier with his well-rounded knowledge of the dope game. He often cut and tested the product.

This day was Karen's second on her return. She had a lot of money on hand. Only two people knew she was there, Dollar Bill and Quana. Karen begged her daughter not to say anything to her brother, Barry. Quana promised not to. However, Quana's trust came with conditions. She mandated her mom to stay in the apartment and not run the streets. Quana also demanded Karen maintain control of her jonesing and drug habit.

A deal was made between the mother and daughter. Quana even gave her extra cash to keep her situated inside Dollar Bill's spot. She didn't want Karen to leave out for anything. That was an easy thing because all Karen honestly wanted to do was be there in the company of her sibling and the both of them get higher than high could get. Not to mention, her and Dollar Bill had already gone through a large quantity of grams of the potent shit he once so happily bragged about. She could hardly wait to load her veins and relapse with this strain of heroin that was in limited supply. If only Murder knew what his mother was up to.

Karen and Dollar Bill were seated on the patchy carpeted floor of his dingy, sparsely furnished, smoke filled living room, preparing a fix. It was the summer, June, and hot. Dollar Bill had no AC unit in the apartment, only medium sized rotating fans. The twins were sweating like crazy, but still going in. doing the very thing they liked to do.

"Dollar Bill," Karen called out to him. She used her words to indicate the level of fun she was having. "This goddamn Cobra Venom you spoke so much about is some really good shit, like you said it was."

"I told you, didn't I? Shit so goddamn good, it made your ass come outta retirement to know what it was like." Dollar Bill shot back in response. Then he stabbed his arm with the tip of the needle. The syringe was loaded with smack.

Once injecting, he then began to nod and grope on himself from the euphoric feeling the brown sugar colored narcotic caused, it turned this color when heated.

Karen followed his lead and then did the same thing. She pricked her vein and shot a round into her body. A long paused occurred. Karen then slurred out a sentence.

"Dollar Bill, I thought you said... said you had something important to talk with me about?" She managed to get out.

"Yeah, baby girl. I do. I was just waiting for the right time to do so. And I guess now would be a good opportunity for us to talk."

"Mm-hmm. It would," Karen replied.

"I really don't know how to say this, so I'mma just come on out and say it. Okay," he said to place her on notice. He wanted her to be aware of the serious nature of all he had to say.

Karen relaxed her arms and allowed her hands to hit her thighs. She then locked in on her brother with a concerned stare.

"What's up, Dollar Bill. Talk to me bro," she urged him.

"I tested positive for HIV about a year ago," he revealed.

Karen couldn't hold back the emotions. She began to cry, like she hadn't in a very long time.

Dollar Bill attempted to ease her pain with his words. He'd already accepted his fate of whatsoever was to be. "Come on now, Karen. I don't need you doing that crying shit over me, no more than I plan to do so myself. Get it together. We don't need this."

"How that happen, bro?" she asked.

"It had to be from behind one of them dirty needles. Cause I ain't put my wing-wany raw up in no funky whores. I can tell you that much," he responded.

"And how long they say you had it?"

"The doctor say I've been infected maybe two years now. So hey, it is what it is now, sis. I'mma be alright, though. They gave me some pills I supposed to be taking. But I don't. And I get a disability check every month. That's how I'm able to do my thing like I do. You already know me, Karen, find the best supply, get high, and stay that way," Dollar Bill joked.

Both of them burst into laughter at his witty wise-crack.

"Well, you sound like you're in good spirit," Karen said. Her tone more lifted now.

Dollar Bill held up all his paraphernalia and made a comment.

"How can I not be in good spirits, sis? With all these heavenly gifts I got at my disposal here, my spirits are gonna always be good, baby girl. Always," he harmonized once more, and made her laugh yet again.

The two prepared another fix and continued to pump powerful narcotics into their bodies. Dollar Bill had the opportunity he long wanted, to see his twin after nearly five years of her being away from home. Karen's presence and conversation was much needed and appreciated, he thought a little better being able to explain to her what was troubling him. They were good to go, shooting up with some of the best dope Philly had to offer, on a limited basis. They were talking shit, laughing, and having a good time. What more could either of the two ask for? He was good with all he had going on, despite the depressing diagnosis of the illness. Dollar Bill was going to continue being Dollar Bill.

* * * *

Felicia Martinez, the ex-girlfriend of Murder and now AUSA in the Philly jurisdiction, had a few days off from work. She was up early in the A.M. like always, straightening out her apartment and deciding on what she may want to do for the day. It was the Saturday and the weather was on point for a fun outing.

Weeks prior, her and her high school sweetheart reconnected after a decade and more of not seeing or hearing from one another. And just like that, his very sight and refined appearance triggered those uncontrollable yearnings, and powerful emotions overtook her absolute soul.

Felicia seated herself on the black leather love seat in her living room, picked up her phone and sent Murder a text message. She made it her business to keep his number, for a reason. Her desire was to add meaning to her life again.

Felicia: Hello, Barry. How are you?

It took him nearly five minutes to reply. She knew him well enough to know exactly what he was up to at eight o'clock a.m on Saturday morning. Murder was out for a jog. He always preferred this type of physical activity on the weekends. This routine dated back to high school, when he was on the track and basketball teams.

Barry: Hey, Felicia. I'm good. Out for a jog now. I just put my ear piece in. Call me, let's talk.

She hit the call icon on her phone. He answered.

"Hey. How you been?"

"I'm well, Barry. Was tidying up my place and the thought of you came across my mind. I thought it would be a good time to contact you early, like I am now, to possibly set up something for us to get into today, if you're not too busy with other plans, of course," Felicia suggested.

"Oh, no doubt. We could definitely do something today. I don't have much on my schedule to take care of. Besides, on Saturdays, it's usually at night," he responded.

"Right. Things related to your business as a night life mogul, correct?"

"Absolutely. That's what I do now. I'm into night life activities. I'm into partying and entertainment, and I'm into promotions, hence the name *Murdoch Entertainment and Promotions*. That me."

Murder was happy to reiterate his new position. This was a far cry from the ordinary street punk he was viewed as by her father, who became vehement in anger at the fact of his daughter being involved with him. He often ran Murder out of the house and away from his baby girl. But no matter what, Papa Bear couldn't keep her away from the bad boy she loved in Barry. Felicia was obsessed with him and his mystique. And there was nothing no one could say or do about it.

"What's a good time for us to hook up?" She asked, temporarily reverting to how she used to talk with him, instead of her professional disposition.

"About three will be good. Once I'm done with my workout, I gotta stop by the barber shop to get a cut and beard line up. One more stop after that, then to my place I go to shower, get dressed, and meet up with you. What you had in mind to do? Where would you like to go?" Murder asked of his first love.

"Well, you know I love to be outside, enjoying walks, visiting an ice cream parlor for the best flavors, or to a café for a float and onion rings. I wouldn't mind exploring the possibility of us having our old thing back, at least for a few hours," Felicia revealed her true desire.

"I wouldn't mind either, sweetie. I'll hit you up once I'm done. Okay."

"Alright, I'll be waiting."

The call ended.

The two returned to doing as they were before the conversation initiated.

Chapter 20

Seven Hours Later . . .

The two former lovebirds, Felicia and Murder, were seated at the Hard Rock café, enjoying onion rings, chicken tenders, and their favorite flavor float, strawberry.

"Felicia, listen. I've mentioned a lot about myself to you, but you haven't told me exactly what you do for living," Murder pointed out.

His desire was to know the progress that she'd made through the years.

"I'm an attorney now, Barry. I practice law," Felicia responded.

"Oh really? A lawyer?" Murder was impressed at her achievement.

"Mm-hmm, an officer of the court."

"Wow. That's amazing. It really is. I'm proud of you, Felicia. I really, really am. As much as you used to argue at me for not calling some days, or for being out and about with my boys and you not having any idea where I used to be, to become a lawyer was only fitting for you," he said and chuckled behind his remark.

They sat along the row of counter seats as they ate and reminisced. Felicia found humor and delight in his remarks. She turned her head to face him. They locked eyes. She pursed her lips, then returned a smile of her own to display the pleasure felt.

"Becoming a lawyer was only fitting for me, you say, huh? Since I loved to argue at you," she retorted with a smile.

Murder smiled brightly himself, tossed his hands midway into the air, and made an additional comment to support the exchange of pleasantries. "Hey, I'm just saying. You would argue like hell at me, in English and Spanish. Cursing my behind out, and telling me you love me so much, all at the same time," he let out, still smiling, showing all thirty-two teeth.

Murder continued on with his humorous speech. "You finally made it your business to teach me a basic level of Spanish, so I could know what all you were saying," he said, and followed up with a laugh.

"You still remember your Spanish lessons I taught you?" Felicia asked.

"Oh, absolutely I do. How could I forget? I went on to take a few advance courses after the fact. I'm fluent with it now."

Felicia held an elongated glance and smile at Murder, while thinking up something to say in Spanish so as to put him to the test. She then spoke in her native tongue.

"Barry, I never lost my love for you. I always maintained high hopes that we would eventually get back together in life and live the dream of a power couple as we always desired," she said.

"And I never lost my love or affection for you either, Felicia. I too, have and will always love you, and kept the hope in mind that we would get back together," he responded in Spanish, precisely.

They both leaned in at the same time and began to tongue kiss. The few other patrons there looked on at them and smiled. They wished for the best for Barry and Felicia.

If all was to continue to go well, how would he balance his dealings with the multiple females he had? He was now faced with one hell of a conundrum to figure out, and a limited amount of time to do so, being that Charlotte now strongly considered moving to Philly, all on account of him. Also, Brooklyn, being a young hot ticket herself, demanded her respect, along with more of his attention. Now Felicia was back on the scene, spraying a mist of her love ether onto a flame of passion and desire they both possessed. It was a must for him to figure things out.

They left Hard Rock and made their way to the piers at Penn's Landing for a stroll along the Delaware River. They held hands and got deep into conversation, once more.

There was a vendor present. He had a push car loaded with merchandise, key chains, car mirror hangers, decorated ink pens, phone cases, and other objects. Murder and Felicia bought matching key chains that had a heart and shark amulets on them.

"May these chains hold the keys to our hearts and a life that's to be filled with prosperity," Felicia stated.

"And may these sharks eat us up, if we fail to pursue the life and the dream, we once desired together, and now have the opportunity to make a reality," Murder stated as they exchanged gifts.

Felicia repeated his words as they proposed a toast, by tapping the ornaments together.

The conversation of the two continued, making each other aware of all they'd done throughout the years.

"So once you graduated high school and left, where did you go?" Murder asked. He was curious to know. He had no knowledge.

"I thought I mentioned that to you already." She had, but very briefly. Felicia had a lot to hide from him.

"You may have. But I feel like I missed something in between. Our love was so strong, for you to have simply up and left on me like that," Murder said to her. "At least I thought that anyway."

"Our love was strong, Barry. However, I had a career to pursue, a father whose health was beginning to fail, and my immediate family to take care of. So I had a future and more people to think about than myself and you, and all it was we wanted. Nonetheless, you wanted to know where I went. I don't mind sharing that with you," Felicia stated. She then went on to give him a brief synopsis of her journey.

They had a photographer take a few photos of them hugging, kissing, and expressing affection for one another. They were on the crossing over pass of I-95 that stretched from Penn's Landing to South Street. The pictures were lovely.

The two then strolled up the famous South Street shopping strip. They made a stop at Him and Her Boutique and at a fragrance haven, then strolled back down on the opposite side. The time was nearing 7:00 pm, they'd been out for hours together. Felicia wanted to spend more time with him. However, Murder had an important meeting to get to. Herb texted him and demanded they talk in person. It was about business.

"I'm hoping we could do more of this, often, Felicia. I really enjoyed the time out. In a way, it feels like we never were apart. But I got to go. I've got some business to attend to. Okay," he made her aware.

"It's okay. I understand. Go do what you have to do. And yes, we can do this again soon. I'd love to. I'm almost always available on the weekends."

"You said that like you're a hopeless romantic or something, girl," he remarked, then chuckled.

"I may as well be. All I do is work long hours of the day, go home, work more while I'm home, go out on occasion with a friend I have, and spend time with my sister and family. That's it. The wonderful life of Felicia Martinez, a woman with a professional life and no kids," she responded, nonchalantly running through her day-to-day life.

"So, I assume, this is the first time in a long time you've had a chance to get out and do something like this, huh?" Murder asked. He dug in with the question to know more about the friend she mentioned.

"When a woman dates a guy who works at the same place she does, and they basically do the same thing, the life I have is the result of that." Felicia confirmed the suspicions he had.

Murder took a look at his watch. Time was moving fast from his perspective.

"Felicia, look, I've gotta go, okay. Would you like for me to take you home?" he asked.

They were at the corner of South Street and 8th Avenue, awaiting the traffic light to change and the vehicles to pass.

"No, no. I'm good. You go on ahead. I can take a taxi or an Uber from here. I really enjoyed your time today, Barry," she said with a bright smile. "Made me feel special again."

"Special enough to move that little friend of yours out the way, I hope." He spoke direct on what his intentions now were.

"The possibilities are endless, my dear. The possibilities are endless," Felicia expressed. The catchy phrase was so nice, she felt the need to repeat herself.

"Be sure to call me soon, okay," he lastly said, then leaned down and pecked her on the lips.

"Don't worry. I will."

Murder then walked away, headed back to his car that was parked down at Penn's Landing.

Felicia wanted badly to let Murder know that she'd be glad to have him take her home. However, two main reasons prevented that, the safety and privacy policy as an AUSA, and she didn't want to run the risk of being recognized by someone who put her in harm's way, or worse, endangered her life.

In the future, there may definitely be a need for Felicia to reveal the fact that she was a prosecuting lawyer, and responsible for putting people in prison. People like him, who were involved in the criminal world.

Of course, her decision would have to be based on whether or not she wanted to continue moving forward with him and re-establish in their adult life what they had as teenagers. Things were looking pretty good so far. The flame of love was rekindled and burned brightly.

Chapter 21

One Hour Later...
Murder made his way to meet up with Herb. They had some pressing business that needed to be discussed. A potential new connect, one that would supply a large quantity of product, except it wouldn't be heroin. The potential connection was into the opioid, meth, and designer drug market. The use thereof and the amount of the money made from these new age products had a steady rise in pace. Not to mention, the fact that a tremendous percentage of opioid based narcotics in America was legalized for pharmaceutical distribution. Herb was convinced that this was now the way to turn as a dealer. He wanted it no other way.

The two friends met at the studio they owned together. The small office served as a conference room, where they often held conversations.

"Herb, what's good, bro? How you been? We ain't had the chance to link up in a minute. Tell me something good," Murder said to initiate the talk.

"Shit bro, I'm doing all I can to make things good again on my end. Been making crazy progress lately," Herb responded.

"I hope you have some information about those fifteen bricks that was stolen from us included in that progress, my nigga! Because, if somebody got us like that, the very last of all we had at the moment, then what else might they know?

138

Who could it have been? Shit. For all we know, it could've been a motherfucka' who may be looking to take aim and kill us next, if they not able to catch us slipping again with product to steal. Think about that bro," Murder said what was on his mind in a serious tone.

"Bro. You don't think I wish I knew who the motherfucka' is that snaked us out our shit? I'd put a bullet in their head myself. Won't need no hitter to do it, I'd handle that. But I'm in the blind, too. I don't have no idea. And we ain't got no way to find out any faster who done it. So what other options we got than to simply move on? You tell me."

"I'm just saying, bro. That was over a half million dollars worth of product we gotta let go just like that. We came a long way, Herb, to get that shit, and left a trail of bodies and everything else along the way. And you already know, I'm not the one to let shit go easily," Murder stated.

He was clearly pissed and wanted smoke behind somebody stealing from them.

Herb pursed his lips and shrugged his shoulders. "What more can we do, Murder? I lost half the money. We paid for the product, too. But I understand that's part of the game, bro. We can't continue to cry over spilled milk. We got to move forward. And that's what I wanted to talk to you about, us moving forward."

Herb was successful in finding a way to help Murder see things for what they truly were, a loss. That was all there was to it.

Murder exhaled heavily. He hated to be defeated in anything, including being persuaded to let things go. Those were two things he despised with a passion, losing and rejection. And losing fifteen kilos of heroin to a thief, on top of his business partner telling him they needed to let it go, tormented him to hell and back. This was so because he couldn't make it his business to get even.

Murder raised his hands in surrender and let them fall freely to the wayside, slapping himself on the thighs as he plopped into the seat of the desk chair. "I guess you right, Herb. What the fuck can we do other than move on? So what's on the table now? What you got?" Murder asked.

"What I got? Information you may want to consider. A possible new connect," Herb mentioned.

"Talk to me," Murder urged.

"Ok, look. You know my Russian dude who keep us supplied with the guns, right? Vladimir?"

"No doubt. What he talking 'bout?"

"Him and his people pushing heavy material in two areas. They got weapons. And they got top quality designer pills. They are looking to expand. And need additional distros."

"You mean they trying to get a hand in on money that's to be made in the black underworld, don't you?" Murder retorted.

"Well, if you wanna put it that way, then yeah, that's what I meant. Anyway, they're the ones who got the product. They need dealers to add to the network and to move the product," Herb said.

"Herb. Look. Grade A quality heroin is our product, bro, and we are already part of a network. Why do we need to break from that to try something new? I don't understand."

"Because, bro, if we had heroin to sell, then we wouldn't be in this predicament anyway. And why should we continue to be a part of a network where we got a hitter on the loose, a bitch in a skirt, who's wreaking havoc on everybody, and no one seems to have any idea who's behind it? Not to mention, the fact that this current network ain't provide any product since God knows when. How you justify that, my nigga?"

Herb made a solid point. His intentions were to make it hard for Murder to dispute the change in direction he wanted to make.

"We need to make money, bro, like yesterday."

His facetious rhetoric stung Murder in a raw way. The reality of not having any product and having not made any money off drug deals for a prolonged period of time caused Murder to consider switching up, but not make a definite decision, at least not yet. He still maintained the hope that his agreement with Major would come to be at some point soon, and he'd finally have the opportunity to be introduced to Ruiz. And now that he knew the whole story behind it all, and also who was the mastermind running the show, why would he jump ship and join another team? To Murder, that would be an act of treason, especially since he'd killed to be a part of his current network, one his very own brother was the head nigga in charge of. Jabari was the one whom put Murder in the position he held and helped him make the type of money to enjoy his luxurious lifestyle.

"Herb. Real talk, bro. I couldn't join another network, not even if I wanted to. I'm in too deep already with the current regime. It's a lot you don't know anything about," he stated, reiterating his position.

"That's all good and dandy for you, bro. You're the one in too deep, as you put it, not me. I gotta eat, too. I gotta make a way for myself. I can't continue to pass up opportunities, waiting on our current supplier to make their mind up to provide us with more work. I need to make progress. You feel me? I know we entered this dark world together. And we've been tight long before it all. But I think we are at a crossroad now, bro, as far as being business partners in the game is concerned. I can't see myself passing up this opportunity, bro. I can't afford to." Herb gave straightforward clarity on the position he now took.

"I tell you what, bro. Because you're the only one who's close to me in this shit, I know I can trust you. You've been my brother since we had skid marks in our Thunder Cat drawers, running wild." They both had to laugh at his remark before he continued. "This is what I can do. Because you seem to be determined to move in a different direction with the product your Russian people holding onto."

"The dope game is beginning to play out, bro. The new shit is what's happening now."

Murder thought, I really don't wanna think in this way. But I'm starting to feel like my homie, Herb, had everything to do with those last fifteen bricks being stolen from us. This nigga dead serious about getting out the heroin business and moving on to something else. Why else would he, all of a sudden, be bringing to my attention anything about a proposition dealt to him from a whole different network, that has another type of product we don't deal in? It's too much of a coincidence here for him to not be guilty of something. I plan to get down to the bottom of it, though, no matter what.

Murder thought long and deep to himself before responding. "I beg to differ on that, bro. The dope game is still alive and well, last I checked. But what I was saying was that I can't hold you back from the opportunity you've been offered by a guy you know. What I can do is this. Once you get in good with them, and they supply you and increase your buying power. From there we can put people in place to move the product. And if I'm convinced that this new wave is the one to ride, then I'll come all the way on board. How does that sound?

Murder left the door open between them for the possibility of what could be. Also, he was wise enough to not break the bond he and his friend had. No amount of narcotics was strong enough to separate them.

"That sounds like a plan, bro. I'm still my own man. And we still tight as homies. It's win-win for the both of us."

They both smiled and shook hands in agreement. A deal was in place.

"And when the time is right, I'll be sure to let you know all I know about what's really going on with the original supplier. A'ight," Murder said.

"That's what up." Herb acknowledged.

"But on another note, I know you done made progress with that chick, Imani, ain't you?" Murder asked with a smile. He wanted to continue to lighten the mood by talking about females.

"Bro, have I? Progress ain't even the word for that. We're prospering like no other."

The two friends continued to talk and enjoy the company of one another.

Chapter 22

Gustavo Ruiz was now back into the habit of conducting business. He was eager to open the pipeline once again and unleash the heroin product onto the streets of America. He was safely tucked away in his native country, Colombia, out of harm's way of the authorities.

A meeting was being held between him and the US distributors. There were two from each state he supplied, California, Texas, New York, and Pennsylvania. Ruiz was specifically concerned with his Philly distro network, and there sat Felipe Valdez and Major Appleton to properly explain to him the whole ordeal that played out along the food chain there. Their hopes were to unclog the heroine pipeline and make the dope flow once more.

"So, gentleman, I am so happy to have you here at my home, here in Colombia, to enjoy the lovely weather, and all I have lined up for you over the weekend," Ruiz said.

It was a Friday afternoon. The visitors were set to leave by private jet to Miami the following Monday.

"And we're happy to be here with you, Señor. It's an honor," responded Major and Highway, seemingly at the same time.

"I'm aware I've explained this to you once before, and delighted to do so yet again," said Ruiz. "Personally, I deal with niggers. I deal with wetbacks. And I deal with the low end of my own Colombian people. To me, blacks in the United States, Mexicans, Puerto Ricans, Dominicans, and

144

Panamanians are all one and the same. I want their money. And at the same time, I want control over the very souls. How do I have them both? It's simple with the product that I provide. I could give a rat's ass about anything other than that. Do you all understand my point?"

The arrogance and conscienceless regard for humanity came out of Ruiz. He'd transformed into the drug dealing tyrant that the American federal government deemed him to be. And they were desperate to nab him and put him away forever.

Major and Highway were completely unfazed by the racial insults, although directed at them.

"We understand, Señor," Highway said.

"Yeah. Your point is understood. You want your money regardless of whom or what," Major chimed in. "And the users of your product will do whatever necessary to get their hands on it, even if it means to sacrifice their souls to do so."

"You have good insight, Major. Way to go," responded Ruiz. "Okay, now that we have begun this meeting, I want to specifically continue on to tell you two, Major and Felipe, how we shall do business moving forward. I have designed a new protocol for my Philadelphia distro network. Being that the majority of my California operations were shut down for many reasons, this means that my east coast production rate will pick up with double the amount than before," Ruiz explained.

"Double the amount?" Major was the first to protest. "How are we supposed to establish that type of clientele and we haven't had any product to sell in quite some time now? Not only that, how are we supposed to come up with the money to cover the overhead prices on the additional amount of kilos you want to overload us with?"

"Yeah, Señor. I don't understand," Highway spoke up. "How do you expect us to place that type of demand on our crew on such a short notice?"

"If you two let me finish, I'll explain," Ruiz retorted. He continued, "My intention is to grant you additional time to make adjustments and to increase your output, so as to sell my heroin product in the time frame which I expect."

"Ok. Good. And when are we going to get the supply you speak of, so that our crew can get busy getting rid of it? That's what I'm trying to know. Because patience has near ran out with my people. And they're demanding answers from me," Major wanted to know.

The dealers along his network, Murder and C-Ro, had really gotten antsy with him. Money needed to be made before the workers jumped ship and move on to another distribution team, something Herb had already done.

"No need to worry, my friends. Everything is fine. I had to assure myself that the authorities were not following you. I'd gotten word from one of my men on the inside that a worker of mine turned informant for the government. And I don't have any idea what he may have told, or what they know," stated Ruiz, tossing his hands in the air midway.

"So we don't have to wait for product any longer, I assume?" Felipe asked.

"Your assumptions are correct, Felipe. You have to wait no more. By the time you make it back to your city, my heroin product shall be there awaiting your pick up. And then you and Major can pay me my money. The single most material thing that I love so dearly, American currency. My safety had to come first. And as long as I'm not on American soil, the US Officials have no jurisdiction. No jurisdiction means that their investigation is limited. Once you two make your return, I have a watchman in place, who shall now oversee the operation. This person will be responsible for collecting my money and will also let me know when more product is needed. Do you both understand?"

Gustavo spoke in a clear and decisive tone. He wanted to ensure there was no misunderstanding. He demanded compliance and loyalty.

Major and Felipe both agreed to everything Gustavo detailed. Although the both had too much going on in their own camps, in and around Philly, they knew, without a doubt, that things would be manageable once the product begin to circulate once more and everyone was making money.

Gustavo treated his guest lavishly for the next three days. They were offered the opportunity to indulge into every type of top-quality vice that Colombia had to offer, especially the exotic and beautiful working girls of the country. Gustavo had the best of them. But for the most part, the men drank the plentiful alcohol available, smoked on the most exclusive cigars, and partied with the girls all night and day at the resort where they stayed. Business was now good again and Gustavo was looking to prosper.

With the sale of his heroin product bringing in more money again, Gustavo could now buy more guns and weapons from his Russian and Israeli business partners, arm his civilian rebels to fight against the government of Colombia, and continue to fund the on-going war being fought. His interest and determination were to protect those natural resource mines from the hands and agenda of the corrupt politicians and law makers, who had intentions to do other things with the material drawn from them, especially those cobalt mines the country was rich with. Gustavo and several other narcotic drug lords were joined at the hip and fought alongside one another, battle after battle, as the war rolled on. At all cost, they intended to win.

Chapter 23

Both Charlotte and her colleague friend, Imani, had the weekend off from work at the hospital. They wanted to treat themselves to a Saturday at the spa for massages, manicures and pedicures. The two ladies hadn't truly had the opportunity to hang out lately and get really deep into the type of girl talk that they desired. The phone conversations were good. However, it wasn't anything like being able to discuss how life was going in person. They loved to play off the energy and body language of each other. And what better way to do so than at an exclusive high-end massage spa, pampering themselves.

Charlotte laid down to rest on the cushioned spa chair as a female therapist squeezed warm oil all over her body to relieve the tension she experienced. Charlotte's left arm hung low, flashing the five carat jewel that her significant other provided. The smile on her face hadn't gone away since the day she received it.

The particular massage parlor they visited was one they were very familiar with. They had been there a few times in the past and loved the hospitality of the staff. Their usual therapists weren't available to attend to Charlotte and Imani, they had high profile appointments to satisfy. They were told a couple of professional athletes were their exclusive clientele. Nonetheless, the two new female therapists who treated the two medical professions were just as trained and qualified as the others Charlotte and Imani had a rapport with.

A conversation with an interesting topic began between the two, one Charlotte absolutely wanted to have.

"Mani, Remember I mentioned to you about the dinner Barry and I were invited to?" Charlotte began.

"I do. But you never spoke on the details of it. Did y'all attend?" Imani responded.

"Ooh, yes, we did attend. And I'm thankful that we did. Turns out, baby boy, Barry, had a little more clout and money, might I add, than I initially gave him credit for. And this was also the same night he gave me this here ring," she said, smiling like a Chester cat and lifting her hand to express her point. Basically, rubbing in how well her and Murder were doing.

"Oh, yeah. And how is that? More clout and money?"

"Well, we had dinner at the home of a prominent city councilman and his wife."

"A city councilman and his wife? Really? That's somebody with a little power, isn't it? They got a lot of influence in many ways, too. And being in Philadelphia, a city councilman, the fifth largest city in the country, that's a huge step in the right direction for you two."

"Yep. It definitely is. He's a well loved and respected city councilman, too. I looked him up. His name is Major and his wife's name is Lori. They have an amazing home, too, girl. You should see it. It's a two-story mansion with a pool in the back. Lovely as ever, it's a bite size piece of heaven, in my opinion," Charlotte explained.

She then had a thought on how nice life must be for the two, in their private affair and in the eyes of the public.

"The Appletons, have a legit way of how they conduct business and carry themselves, a life worth living, Something I would love to finally be able to enjoy."

Before Charlotte's previous way of living fell apart and went to hell, she did have a nice home, one better than what

Lori now had. She drove a nice luxury vehicle, better that what Lori now drove. She wore top dollar designer labels in clothes, more expensive than the tags Lori popped herself. She went on shopping sprees, dined at the best spots, and took lavish vacations to many destination of her choice. She'd gone practically everywhere but to the Vatican City, the home seat of the Pope. She felt as though she wasn't welcomed there to spend the blood stained drug money of her boyfriend. With Reign man, Charlotte had many of the finer things that life had to offer. However, the problem was there wasn't any legitimacy to the money that he had. At the time, she wasn't smart enough to know how to clean it up and make it right, at least for her and their daughter, little Ni'Asia.

Now that she had Murder in her life, a version of her ex but wiser in how he moved and did things, she was determined to get it right this time around, and that meant all across the board with it. She wasn't going to lose out anymore. This is what she repeatedly told herself.

The conversation continued to get deeper.

"I'm sure you and Barry must've really enjoyed yourselves," Imani said.

"Oh girl. Did we ever? To be totally honest with you, I have never done something like that before. You know, dealing with the high profile, respected couple, at least not in such a private setting. Barry had me fooled, yet again. I thought he may turn out to be more of a street thug. What a way to lie and disguise himself," Charlotte stated.

"Barry seems to keep pulling one over on you, in a good way, Charlotte. But is it you who had it all wrong all this time? I'm only going out." She had a chuckle with her words.

"He does seem to continue in pulling one over on me. And you're right, it was me," she said, shaking her head at herself in pleasant disbelief and smiling at the same time. She continued. "Although his presence, his demeanor, and, at

THESE VICIOUS STREETS 2 | PRINCE A. TAUHID

times, attire may seem street to you, that dude is such the gentleman, Mani. Lord knows he is."

Charlotte cherished the knowledge of all she knew. Murder was in private the many things nobody knew of him, except her.

"I believe there is more to it than you're telling me, boo. I know you, Charlotte. Go ahead and spill the beans. He wants to move in with you, here in DC, doesn't he?" Imani asked as she probed deeper.

"It's not Barry," Charlotte stated.

"It is not Barry?" Imani asked, picking up on the tone Charlotte spoke in. "You got somebody else I don't know about?"

"No, Mani. Don't be ridiculous, girl," Charlotte let out playfully.

"Well which one of you contemplating a life changing move then?"

"If you must know, Lori, the wife of the councilman, she and I were really able to connect. We talked amongst ourselves as we toured their home, while Barry and her husband had a private meeting. Lori took a liking to me. Apparently, she's one of the head members of the social society called Elite Women of Philadelphia. I researched her. Those ladies have a lot of power, and a lot of influence, as well, in the areas that matter most."

"You mean important areas that matter most, like in their bedrooms, pillow talking with their powerful husbands," Imani retorted in a joking manner.

Charlotte had to laugh at the remark. It had a humorous punch to it.

"Yeah, that too. But this group of *bougie* whores has a lot of pull, mane. By me connecting with Lori, I can use the power of the group for what it's worth, to continue to get ahead," Charlotte stated.

"So, this Lori female, invited you to join?"

151

"She's the one who made me aware of a spot opening in the circle of ladies that she's the leader of. She wants me to have it."

"And what did you say to that?" Imani asked.

"I told her I'd get back to her about it soon, being that it's a requirement to go along with the membership."

"Well I'm smart enough to know that the name of the group is Elite Women of Philadelphia. You live here in DC. So I assume that the requirement you spoke of is for you to move from here to there?" Imani said, then got silent to await Charlotte's response.

"You're right. It's gonna require me to move to Philly to join the group, a move I don't believe I'll have a problem with," Charlotte confirmed.

"But what about your position at the hospital?"

"Lori has already assured me that she knows people in that area who'll help with the transfer. And I wouldn't mind getting on at the Children's hospital there. Shriners, is one of the top medical facilities in the country. There's only a few of them. Philly happens to have one."

"So, what, you plan to just grab Asia, and you and her up and leave town on me and Farrah? We don't get to see you two but a few times a month. That's how you'll do us?" Imani made her case. She wanted her friend, Charlotte, to stay close, at least for the sake of the girls. She didn't want to separate them by the five-hour distance between DC and Philly. The two were like sisters.

"Mani, if anybody, you know my intentions are always good. And I wouldn't make no plans of my own without being sure that I put you and Farrah somewhere into the equation. Also, as good as you've spoken lately about the progress you and Herb are making, I would've thought it would be you who was looking to make the transition to Philly first, not me," Charlotte stated.

Imani smiled at her words and at the thought of Herb. "You make a good point. And true indeed, me and Herb have made progress, tremendous progress. I don't think it's too early for me to say that I believe he may be my soulmate. I only need to feel him out a little more to confirm a thing or two. But a move away from here could be a good thing. Hell, I've been here my whole life. Change is always good, anytime a person has been complacent for far too long. And that's me, here in DC," Imani expressed her openness to change.

"So exactly what are you trying to say, Mani? That, yes, you're willing to move? Is that what you're saying to me?" Charlotte asked, looking at Imani in the eyes as they lay next to one another on the massage table.

"That's exactly what I'm saying, boo. So you go ahead, lock in with your new groupie, Lori, the wife of the councilman, and let her help you make a smooth transition. Then, once you're properly situated, I'll be right behind you with my move, and you can help me do the same. If Lori, with the power and the influence, wants to be your friend, then let her. It's always good to have friends in high places, my girl. And not only that, you'll really know what's going on full time with Barry, once you're there. You'll see whether he's ready to embrace being Barry, the businessman, or if he wants to continue being Murder, the street thug. So, I highly encourage you to go ahead and make the move, sweetie. And in due time, we may be able to have a home in the same neighborhood." Imani provided her honest thoughts and suggestions on the subject.

"A'ight if this is something you'll support, then this is something I'll do. It makes all the sense to me to do so. I don't see why not. I just need to run it by Barry first."

Imani cut her sentence short. "Charlotte, no. Don't mention anything to him, just simply do it. I'm sure he'll respect it. Besides, he bought you that ring, didn't he? To me, that's a sign he wants to be close anyway. Both if you are going in opposite directions than me and Herb are."

"How you figure that?'

"Because Barry busy chasing you. He's up your ass. And with us, I'm busy chasing Herb. I'm the one on his dick. In other words, it's you who dictate what's to go in y'all relationship. And it's Herb to do that with us, just the way I want it. You get it?" Imani laid out her perspective of things in plain language for her friend.

"Yeah, I guess I do. But all I want to know is, if I go to do this move, do you promise to do the same in due time?" Charlotte asked. "You're not gonna stand me up, are you?"

"You have my word, Charlotte. I'm moving once you do so. Okay? I promise. And you need to be sure to utilize Lori's phone number and her acquaintance to the best of your ability. The way it sounds is that you have a friend in her, the same as the world does in Jesus," Mani wittily said.

Imani's remark was so striking with wit that it caused the two female massage therapists to laugh out loud. Charlotte and Imani were so deep in conversation and preoccupied with their thoughts that they seemed to have totally forgotten about where they were and what was going on. The four of them now came together to giggle at the humor Imani proudly put on display. She always had a natural way of being calculated in this regard. The moment was won by her.

Epilogue

Throughout the entire time the ladies were at the spa being pampered, there was something more on the side of the investigation going on. Imani wasn't the one who had anything to worry about once revealed. However, the same could not be said about Charlotte. She had a new set of issues developing, of which she had absolutely no knowledge. The two therapists who attended to them were special agents of the FBI.

At the time when Charlotte initiated the international call to her mother, in Trinidad and Tobago, it was discovered by her handlers from the Witness Protection Program. An ongoing investigation by the government, regarding possible tax evasion and other financial schemes of the Margaux family, Charlotte's mother in particular, was never closed. It was the mother whom both Charlotte and her ex-boyfriend, Reign Man, entrusted with large amounts of money, dating back to the day when Reign Man's bodyguard, Threat, shot and killed her cousin, Ralo, and Reign man forced her to go to her native country. Little did he know, Charlotte had transferred $3,000,000 of the $8,000,000 he had in a trust fund for their daughter, Ni'Asia. The account was in Charlotte and her mother's name. In addition, Charlotte took $1,500,000 from the safe in the house. She put that into a bank account in Trinidad and Tobago before Reign Man arrived. He knew nothing.

Charlotte felt that the time was right to now begin spending the money, being that many years had lapsed. This was primarily the reason she contacted her mother when she had. With her in the process of moving to Philadelphia and wanting to buy a new home, the money down in the Caribbean could definitely be useful in many ways.

At the time when Reign Man's home was raided and he was arrested, the money and other valuables he had inside the home were seized, along with the finances he had in the bank. Multiple accounts were discovered. The feds wiped him down clean of all he had. At least all that was in his and Charlotte's names. The money Charlotte's mother maintained in legit accounts down in Trinidad couldn't be touched. The Trinidadian officials didn't allow American officials to fully investigate the citizens of their country. Therefore, the probe into the business affairs of the mother and other Margaux relatives was blocked because they were neither Reign nor Charlotte, and no intrusion into the lives of the other people was tolerated. The concealed escrow accounts Charlotte created were protected, and so was the money her mother held onto for her. A wise move played to perfection by Charlotte.

As it related to the use of female federal agents acting as massage therapists, the Witness Protection Personnel in conjunction with the FBI field office, there in DC, both made it their business to retrieve the phone records of Charlotte and were made aware of her contacting her mother in Trinidad. They were aware of her contact with a couple of numbers that belonged to Philadelphia residents. One number in particular, Murder's phone number, was part of an investigation into a criminal enterprise, as well as the disappearance and possible death by homicide of a federal confidential informant, Montez Shaw, aka "Duck."

The DC feds and Witness Protection Officials immediately began to brainstorm and speculate, the very moment they took notice of Charlotte's particular contacts.

They were now looking to build cases and nail criminals. Not to mention, Barry Murdoch was a guy whom they were aware had pending drug charges that the Philly US Attorney's office was contemplating picking up and prosecuting. They had additional information that linked him to the Shaw CI and now Charlotte, as well. Upon the feds coming into the knowledge of Charlotte's frequent visits to the spa, they felt it was the ideal opportunity to situate their own amongst Charlotte and her friend, to see what all they may have to talk about. It turned out that their play paid off with a plethora of useful information. They were able to pinpoint her by the use of her bank card and cell phone GPS.

As for Murder, he had his cell phone, penthouse lease and residential property he owned in New York City, all under the name of a Brooklyn Carter. And it wasn't a matter of if the feds were going to nab her and put the press down on the girl to talk, but rather when they planned to do so, since timing was a crucial element to it all.

A whole can of worms was opened in the massage parlor that day. Charlotte made the decision to speak loosely to her friend, Imani, and the feds were looking to capitalize from her uncontrolled tongue. Although she didn't know any better and certainly didn't mean any harm, it made no difference what her intentions were to the feds. The golden rule holds true: No matter who you are or what you do, "the less said, is always the best said!" It couldn't have been put any better.

To Be Continued . . .

Lock Down Publications and Ca$h Presents
Assisted Publishing Packages

BASIC PACKAGE $499 Editing Cover Design Formatting	**UPGRADED PACKAGE** $800 Typing Editing Cover Design Formatting
ADVANCE PACKAGE $1,200 Typing Editing Cover Design Formatting Copyright registration Proofreading Upload book to Amazon	**LDP SUPREME PACKAGE** $1,500 Typing Editing Cover Design Formatting Copyright registration Proofreading Set up Amazon account Upload book to Amazon Advertise on LDP, Amazon and Facebook Page

***Other services available upon request.
Additional charges may apply

Lock Down Publications
P.O. Box 944
Stockbridge, GA 30281-9998
Phone: 470 303-9761

Submission Guideline

Submit the first three chapters of your completed manuscript to ldpsubmissions@gmail.com. In the subject line add **Your Book's Title**. The manuscript must be in a Word Doc file and sent as an attachment. Document should be in Times New Roman, double spaced, and in size 12 font. Also, provide your synopsis and full contact information. If sending multiple submissions, they must each be in a separate email.

Have a story but no way to send it electronically? You can still submit to LDP/Ca$h Presents. Send in the first three chapters, written or typed, of your completed manuscript to:

LDP: Submissions Dept
P.O. Box 944
Stockbridge, GA 30281-9998

DO NOT send original manuscript. Must be a duplicate.
Provide your synopsis and a cover letter containing your full contact information.

Thanks for considering LDP and Ca$h Presents.

NEW RELEASES

BLOODLINE OF A SAVAGE 1&2
THESE VICIOUS STREETS 1&2
RELENTLESS GOON
RELENTLESS GOON 2
BY PRINCE A. TAUHID

THE BUTTERFLY MAFIA 1-3
BY FUMIYA PAYNE

A THUG'S STREET PRINCESS 1&2
BY MEESHA

CITY OF SMOKE 2
BY MOLOTTI

STEPPERS 1,2&3
THE REAL BADDIES OF CHI-RAQ
BY KING RIO

THE LANE 1&2
BY KEN-KEN SPENCE

THUG OF SPADES 1&2
LOVE IN THE TRENCHES 2
CORNER BOYS
BY COREY ROBINSON

TIL DEATH 3
BY ARYANNA

THE BIRTH OF A GANGSTER 4
BY DELMONT PLAYER

PRODUCT OF THE STREETS 1&2
BY DEMOND "MONEY" ANDERSON

NO TIME FOR ERROR
BY KEESE

MONEY HUNGRY DEMONS
BY TRANAY ADAMS

Coming Soon from Lock Down Publications/Ca$h Presents

IF YOU CROSS ME ONCE 6
ANGEL V
By Anthony Fields

IMMA DIE BOUT MINE 5
By Aryanna

A THUGS STREET PRINCESS 3
By Meesha

PRODUCT OF THE STREETS 3
By Demond Money Anderson

CORNER BOYS 2
By Corey Robinson

THE MURDER QUEENS 6&7
By Michael Gallon

CITY OF SMOKE 3
By Molotti

CONFESSIONS OF A DOPE BOY
By Nicholas Lock

THA TAKEOVER
By Keith Chandler

BETRAYAL OF A G 2
By Ray Vinci

CRIME BOSS
By Playa Ray

Available Now

RESTRAINING ORDER 1 & 2
By **CA$H & Coffee**

LOVE KNOWS NO BOUNDARIES 1-3
By **Coffee**

RAISED AS A GOON I, II, III & IV
BRED BY THE SLUMS I, II, III
BLAST FOR ME I & II
ROTTEN TO THE CORE I II III
A BRONX TALE I, II, III
DUFFLE BAG CARTEL I II III IV V VI
HEARTLESS GOON I II III IV V
A SAVAGE DOPEBOY I II
DRUG LORDS I II III
CUTTHROAT MAFIA I II
KING OF THE TRENCHES
By **Ghost**

LAY IT DOWN I & II
LAST OF A DYING BREED I II
BLOOD STAINS OF A SHOTTA I & II III
By **Jamaica**

LOYAL TO THE GAME I II III
LIFE OF SIN I, II III
By **TJ & Jelissa**

IF LOVING HIM IS WRONG…I & II
LOVE ME EVEN WHEN IT HURTS I II III
By **Jelissa**

PUSH IT TO THE LIMIT
By **Bre' Hayes**

BLOODY COMMAS I & II
SKI MASK CARTEL I, II & III
KING OF NEW YORK I II, III IV V
RISE TO POWER I II III
COKE KINGS I II III IV V
BORN HEARTLESS I II III IV
KING OF THE TRAP I II
By **T.J. Edwards**

WHEN THE STREETS CLAP BACK I & II III
THE HEART OF A SAVAGE I II III IV
MONEY MAFIA I II
LOYAL TO THE SOIL I II III
By **Jibril Williams**

A DISTINGUISHED THUG STOLE MY HEART I II & III
LOVE SHOULDN'T HURT I II III IV
RENEGADE BOYS 1-4
PAID IN KARMA 1-3
SAVAGE STORMS 1-3
AN UNFORESEEN LOVE 1-3
BABY, I'M WINTERTIME COLD 1-3
A THUG'S STREET PRINCESS 1&2
By **Meesha**

A GANGSTER'S CODE 1-3
A GANGSTER'S SYN 1-3
THE SAVAGE LIFE 1-3
CHAINED TO THE STREETS 1-3
BLOOD ON THE MONEY 1-3
A GANGSTA'S PAIN 1-3
BEAUTIFUL LIES AND UGLY TRUTHS
CHURCH IN THESE STREETS
By **J-Blunt**

CUM FOR ME 1-8
An LDP Erotica Collaboration

BLOOD OF A BOSS 1-5
SHADOWS OF THE GAME
TRAP BASTARD
By **Askari**

THE STREETS BLEED MURDER 1-3
THE HEART OF A GANGSTA 1-3
By **Jerry Jackson**

WHEN A GOOD GIRL GOES BAD
By **Adrienne**

THE COST OF LOYALTY 1-3
By **Kweli**

BRIDE OF A HUSTLA 1-3
THE FETTI GIRLS 1-3
CORRUPTED BY A GANGSTA 1-4
BLINDED BY HIS LOVE
THE PRICE YOU PAY FOR LOVE 1-3
DOPE GIRL MAGIC 1-3
By **Destiny Skai**

A KINGPIN'S AMBITION
A KINGPIN'S AMBITION II
I MURDER FOR THE DOUGH
By **Ambitious**

TRUE SAVAGE 1-7
DOPE BOY MAGIC 1-3
MIDNIGHT CARTEL 1-3
CITY OF KINGZ 1&2
NIGHTMARE ON SILENT AVE
THE PLUG OF LIL MEXICO 1&2
CLASSIC CITY
By **Chris Green**

A GANGSTER'S REVENGE 1-4
THE BOSS MAN'S DAUGHTERS 1-5
A SAVAGE LOVE 1&2
BAE BELONGS TO ME 1&2
A HUSTLER'S DECEIT 1-3
WHAT BAD BITCHES DO 1-3
SOUL OF A MONSTER 1-3
KILL ZONE
A DOPE BOY'S QUEEN 1-3
TIL DEATH 1-3
IMMA DIE BOUT MINE 1-4
By **Aryanna**

A DOPEBOY'S PRAYER
By **Eddie "Wolf" Lee**

THE KING CARTEL 1-3
By **Frank Gresham**

THESE NIGGAS AIN'T LOYAL 1-3
By **Nikki Tee**

GANGSTA SHYT 1-3
By **CATO**

THE ULTIMATE BETRAYAL
By **Phoenix**

BOSS'N UP 1-3
By **Royal Nicole**

I LOVE YOU TO DEATH
By **Destiny J**

I RIDE FOR MY HITTA
I STILL RIDE FOR MY HITTA
By **Misty Holt**

LOVE & CHASIN' PAPER
By **Qay Crockett**

TO DIE IN VAIN
SINS OF A HUSTLA
By **ASAD**

BROOKLYN HUSTLAZ
By **Boogsy Morina**

BROOKLYN ON LOCK 1 & 2
By **Sonovia**

GANGSTA CITY
By **Teddy Duke**

A DRUG KING AND HIS DIAMOND 1-3
A DOPEMAN'S RICHES
HER MAN, MINE'S TOO 1&2
CASH MONEY HO'S
THE WIFEY I USED TO BE 1&2
PRETTY GIRLS DO NASTY THINGS
By **Nicole Goosby**

LIPSTICK KILLAH 1-3
CRIME OF PASSION 1-3
FRIEND OR FOE 1-3
By **Mimi**

TRAPHOUSE KING 1-3
KINGPIN KILLAZ 1-3
STREET KINGS 1&2
PAID IN BLOOD 1&2
CARTEL KILLAZ 1-3
DOPE GODS 1&2
By **Hood Rich**

THE STREETS ARE CALLING
By **Duquie Wilson**

STEADY MOBBN' 1-3
THE STREETS STAINED MY SOUL 1-3
By **Marcellus Allen**

WHO SHOT YA 1-3
SON OF A DOPE FIEND 1-4
HEAVEN GOT A GHETTO 1&2
SKI MASK MONEY 1&2
By **Renta**

GORILLAZ IN THE BAY 1-4
TEARS OF A GANGSTA 1/&2
3X KRAZY 1&2
STRAIGHT BEAST MODE 1&2
By **DE'KARI**

TRIGGADALE 1-3
MURDA WAS THE CASE 1-3
By **Elijah R. Freeman**

SLAUGHTER GANG 1-3
RUTHLESS HEART 1-3
By **Willie Slaughter**

GOD BLESS THE TRAPPERS 1-3
THESE SCANDALOUS STREETS 1-3
FEAR MY GANGSTA 1-5
THESE STREETS DON'T LOVE NOBODY 1-2
BURY ME A G 1-5
A GANGSTA'S EMPIRE 1-4
THE DOPEMAN'S BODYGAURD 1&2
THE REALEST KILLAZ 1-3
THE LAST OF THE OGS 1-3
By **Tranay Adams**

MARRIED TO A BOSS 1-3
By **Destiny Skai & Chris Green**

KINGZ OF THE GAME 1-7
CRIME BOSS 1-3
By **Playa Ray**

FUK SHYT
By **Blakk Diamond**

DON'T F#CK WITH MY HEART 1&2
By **Linnea**

ADDICTED TO THE DRAMA 1-3
IN THE ARM OF HIS BOSS
By **Jamila**

LOYALTY AIN'T PROMISED 1&2
By **Keith Williams**

YAYO 1-4
A SHOOTER'S AMBITION 1&2
BRED IN THE GAME
By **S. Allen**

TRAP GOD 1-3
RICH $AVAGE 1-3
MONEY IN THE GRAVE 1-3
CARTEL MONEY
By **Martell Troublesome Bolden**

FOREVER GANGSTA 1&2
GLOCKS ON SATIN SHEETS 1&2
By **Adrian Dulan**

TOE TAGZ 1-4
LEVELS TO THIS SHYT 1&2
IT'S JUST ME AND YOU
By **Ah'Million**

KINGPIN DREAMS 1-3
RAN OFF ON DA PLUG
By **Paper Boi Rari**

THE STREETS MADE ME 1-3
By **Larry D. Wright**

CONFESSIONS OF A GANGSTA 1-4
CONFESSIONS OF A JACKBOY 1-3
CONFESSIONS OF A HITMAN
By **Nicholas Lock**

I'M NOTHING WITHOUT HIS LOVE
SINS OF A THUG
TO THE THUG I LOVED BEFORE
A GANGSTA SAVED XMAS
IN A HUSTLER I TRUST
By **Monet Dragun**

QUIET MONEY 1-3
THUG LIFE 1-3
EXTENDED CLIP 1&2
A GANGSTA'S PARADISE
By **Trai'Quan**

CAUGHT UP IN THE LIFE 1-3
THE STREETS NEVER LET GO 1-3
By **Robert Baptiste**

NEW TO THE GAME 1-3
MONEY, MURDER & MEMORIES 1-3
By **Malik D. Rice**

CREAM 2-3
THE STREETS WILL TALK
By **Yolanda Moore**

THE STREETS WILL NEVER CLOSE 1-3
By **K'ajji**

LIFE OF A SAVAGE 1-4
A GANGSTA'S QUR'AN 1-4
MURDA SEASON 1-3
GANGLAND CARTEL 1-3
CHI'RAQ GANGSTAS 1-4
KILLERS ON ELM STREET 1-3
JACK BOYZ N DA BRONX 1-3
A DOPEBOY'S DREAM 1-3
JACK BOYS VS DOPE BOYS 1-3
COKE GIRLZ
COKE BOYS
SOSA GANG 1&2
BRONX SAVAGES
BODYMORE KINGPINS
BLOOD OF A GOON
By **Romell Tukes**

CONCRETE KILLA 1-3
VICIOUS LOYALTY 1-3
By **Kingpen**

THE ULTIMATE SACRIFICE 1-6
KHADIFI
IF YOU CROSS ME ONCE 1-3
ANGEL 1-4
IN THE BLINK OF AN EYE
By **Anthony Fields**

THE LIFE OF A HOOD STAR
By **Ca$h & Rashia Wilson**

NIGHTMARES OF A HUSTLA 1-3
BLOOD AND GAMES 1&2
By **King Dream**

GHOST MOB
By **Stilloan Robinson**

HARD AND RUTHLESS 1&2
MOB TOWN 251
THE BILLIONAIRE BENTLEYS 1-3
REAL G'S MOVE IN SILENCE
By **Von Diesel**

MOB TIES 1-7
SOUL OF A HUSTLER, HEART OF A KILLER 1-3
GORILLAZ IN THE TRENCHES
By **SayNoMore**

BODYMORE MURDERLAND 1-3
THE BIRTH OF A GANGSTER 1-4
By **Delmont Player**

FOR THE LOVE OF A BOSS 1&2
By **C. D. Blue**

KILLA KOUNTY 1-5
By **Khufu**

MOBBED UP 1-4
THE BRICK MAN 1-5
THE COCAINE PRINCESS 1-10
STEPPERS 1-3
SUPER GREMLIN 1-4
By **King Rio**

MONEY GAME 1&2
By **Smoove Dolla**

A GANGSTA'S KARMA 1-4
By **FLAME**

KING OF THE TRENCHES 1-3
By **GHOST & TRANAY ADAMS**

THESE VICIOUS STREETS 2 | PRINCE A. TAUHID

QUEEN OF THE ZOO 1&2
By **Black Migo**

GRIMEY WAYS 1-3
BETRAYAL OF A G
By **Ray Vinci**

XMAS WITH AN ATL SHOOTER
By **Ca$h & Destiny Skai**

KING KILLA 1&2
By **Vincent "Vitto" Holloway**

BETRAYAL OF A THUG 1&2
By **Fre$h**

THE MURDER QUEENS 1-5
By **Michael Gallon**

FOR THE LOVE OF BLOOD 1-4
By **Jamel Mitchell**

HOOD CONSIGLIERE 1&2
NO TIME FOR ERROR
By **Keese**

PROTÉGÉ OF A LEGEND 1&2
LOVE IN THE TRENCHES 1&2
By **Corey Robinson**

THE PLUG'S RUTHLESS DAUGHTER
By **Tony Daniels**

BORN IN THE GRAVE 1-3
CRIME PAYS
By **Self Made Tay**

MOAN IN MY MOUTH
By **XTASY**

173

TORN BETWEEN A GANGSTER AND A GENTLEMAN
By **J-BLUNT & Miss Kim**

LOYALTY IS EVERYTHING 1-3
CITY OF SMOKE 1&2
By **Molotti**

HERE TODAY GONE TOMORROW 1&2
By **Fly Rock**

WOMEN LIE MEN LIE 1-4
FIFTY SHADES OF SNOW 1-3
STACK BEFORE YOU SPLURGE
GIRLS FALL LIKE DOMINOES
NAÏVE TO THE STREETS
By **ROY MILLIGAN**

PILLOW PRINCESS
By **S. Hawkins**

THE BUTTERFLY MAFIA 1-3
SALUTE MY SAVAGERY 1&2
By **Fumiya Payne**

THE LANE 1&2
By Ken-Ken Spence

THE PUSSY TRAP 1-5
By **Nene Capri**

DIRTY DNA
By **Blaque**

SANCTIFIED AND HORNY
by **XTASY**

BOOKS BY LDP'S CEO, CA$H

TRUST IN NO MAN
TRUST IN NO MAN 2
TRUST IN NO MAN 3
BONDED BY BLOOD
SHORTY GOT A THUG
THUGS CRY
THUGS CRY 2
THUGS CRY 3
TRUST NO BITCH
TRUST NO BITCH 2
TRUST NO BITCH 3
TIL MY CASKET DROPS
RESTRAINING ORDER
RESTRAINING ORDER 2
IN LOVE WITH A CONVICT
LIFE OF A HOOD STAR
XMAS WITH AN ATL SHOOTER

www.ingramcontent.com/pod-product-compliance
Lightning Source LLC
Chambersburg PA
CBHW070529260626

47161CB00004B/1666